Peace & Health !
(handwritten inscription and signature)

Tess
and the
Highlander

May McGoldrick

M M Books
PO Box 665
Watertown, CT 06795

ISBN: 9781451520989

First published by HarperTeen;
1st Avon Ed edition (October 22, 2002)

Printed in the United States of America

For Cyrus and Sam, our own young heroes...

CHAPTER 1

*The Isle of May, off the Firth of Forth
Scotland, March 1543*

Tess poked at the corpse with a stick and backed away. Her unbound auburn hair, already soaked from the driving rain, whipped across her eyes when she leaned in to look closer.

The Highlander appeared to be dead, but she couldn't be sure. Long, dark blond hair lay matted across his face. She looked at the high leather boots, darkened by the salt water. The man was wearing a torn shirt that once must have been white. A broad expanse of plaid, pinned at one shoulder by a silver brooch, trailed into the tidal pool. From the thick belt that held his kilt in place, a sheathed dirk banged against an exposed thigh.

A dozen seals watched her from the deep water beyond the surf.

With the storm growing increasingly wilder, she stood indecisively over the body. In all the years she'd been on the island, she'd never seen a human wash up before. Certainly, there had been wrecks in the storms that swept in across the open water, and Auld Charlotte and Garth used to find all kinds of things—some valuable and some worthless—cast up on the shores. Never, though, had there been another person—at least, not since the aging husband and wife had found Tess herself eleven years ago.

Tess pushed aside those thoughts now and crouched beside the man, placing a hand hesitantly on his chest. A faint pounding beneath the shirt was the answer to her prayers…and her fears. She didn't want anyone intruding on her island and in her life. At the same time, she could not allow a living thing to die when she could save it. Or him.

5

The surf crashed over the ring of rock that formed the tidal pool, and the young woman pushed herself to her feet. She drew the leather cloak up to shield her face from the stinging spray of wind-driven brine. When she looked back at the body, the wave had pushed the Highlander deeper into the pool, immersing his face.

Tess immediately dropped her stick and lifted his face out of the water. Glancing over her shoulder, she eyed a flat rock at the far side of the pool. It sat higher than the tide generally rose. Rolling him forward slightly, she held him under the arms just as another wave crested the pool's rim. The surge of water lifted the body, and Tess quickly dragged him through the water toward the rock.

He was heavier than she thought he would be. Out of breath, she finally succeeded in getting him partially anchored on the rock.

Auld Charlotte had once told Tess that they'd found her nearly drowned in this same tidal pool. The thought of that now flickered in her mind. She tried to recall the storm and the ship and the day, but those memories had long ago faded into nightmares. Now, it was all buried too deeply within her to recollect. She wondered if it was a day like this one.

The dirk at the Highlander's side caught her eye, and Tess reached down quickly, yanked the weapon from its sheath, and tucked it into her own belt.

The wind was howling, and the salt spray was stinging her face. Tess looked out at the frothy, gray-green sea, hoping to see some boat searching for the Highlander lying unconscious beside her.

If they came, she wouldn't let herself be seen, though. She wanted no news of her presence be carried to the mainland.

She had only been six years old when the ship had sank and she had washed ashore. But the little she allowed herself to remember from the time before that day was too painful. Tess had no desire to face that horrifying past ever again. There was no place else that she ever wanted to be but here. This island was the only home she had left.

For eleven years, the reclusive couple had kept her existence a secret. And now, with both of them dead, she could only pray to continue her life as before, undisturbed.

Her plan was the same as the one she'd followed dozens of times since washing up on this island. Whenever there was a chance of a fishing boat or some pilgrims coming ashore, Garth and Charlotte would trundle Tess off with plenty of food and blankets to the caves on the western shore of the island. She would remain there in safety until all was well and the visitors were gone.

The only difference now was that she would have to use her own judgment about when it would be safe to come out.

Ready to push herself to her feet, a tinge of curiosity made Tess reach and push the Highlander's wet hair out of his face. Instantly, she was sorry for the action, for the man's features took her by surprise. Even unconscious, or perhaps because of it, he was an extremely handsome man. A high forehead, a straight nose, a face devoid of the beard that she'd assumed all Highlanders wore. He had a face not even marred by scars…yet. Only a few scratches and bruises from his time in the surf.

Angry for allowing herself to be distracted, she started to get to her feet, but one foot slipped, and she had to brace a hand on his chest to catch herself.

His eyes immediately opened, and Tess's breath knotted tightly in her chest. Blue eyes the color of a winter sky stared at her from beneath long dark lashes flecked with gold. She didn't blink. She didn't move. Holding her breath, she remained still for the eternity of a moment until he closed them again.

She edged off the rock and ran as fast and as far as her legs would take her.

The taste in Colin Macpherson's mouth was foul as a dried up chamber bucket.

Rolling onto his side, he felt his stomach heave. He tried to push himself up. He couldn't see. As he turned, Colin's hand slipped off cold wet rock, and he tumbled into a shallow pool of water, banging his ribs hard on the stone as he fell.

"Blasted hell," he groaned, pushing himself onto his knees. Holding his head, he blinked a few times, trying to clean the sand and salt out of his eyes.

Rocks. More rocks. And water. And bobbing heads. He pushed back a long, twisted hank of hair that had fallen across his face, obstructing his vision. He tried to focus on the creatures moving on the rocks.

Seals—a dozen or so—were staring at him from the rocks rimming the pool and from the sea beyond. Their brown eyes were dark and watchful. The image of a woman's face immediately flashed before his mind, and he struggled to push himself to his feet. A couple of seals barked a warning to those on shore.

"H…HULLO!" he called out, only to have the surf and the wind slap the greeting back into his face.

His entire body ached. It had taken great effort to get the words out past his raw, scratched throat, but Colin tried again. He was certain someone *had* been there only moments before. Or was it hours?

"HULLO!"

This time a shriek of seabirds was his only answer. Taking in a painful half breath, he tried to move his feet in the shallow pool. They moved, though it felt as if they were made of lead. Colin succeeded in taking only three steps before he had to sit down on the edge of a rock. The world was spinning around in his head.

Water. Rocks. And on each side of the protected tidal pool, rock-studded banks dotted with occasional patches of sea grass sloped upward from the turbulent sea.

The Macpherson ship had been sailing north when the weather had taken a turn for the worse. It shouldn't have been unexpected, though. The Firth of Forth was famous for its foul and quickly changing moods.

Half o'er, half o'er, from Aberdour. It's fifty fathom deep. And there lies good Sir Patrick Spence, with the Scots lords at his feet.

Well, Colin thought, at least he had washed ashore...wherever he was.

The last clear memory that Colin had was shoving one of the sailors to safety in the aft passageway. The lad was nearly unconscious after being slammed against the ship's gunwales as the great vessel had continued to heel before the tempestuous blast of wind.

The storm had come on fast and hard, but they'd been riding it well. Colin and Alexander, his eldest brother, had been standing with the second mate at the tiller when he'd seen the young man go down. The sea sweeping across the deck had nearly carried the lad overboard.

Colin fought the urge to be ill. The foul, salty, bilge taste rose again into his mouth.

The lad had no sooner been secured when Colin had heard the cries of the lookout above. The dark shape of land appeared, not an arrowshot to port. And then the ship's keel had struck the sand bar.

He remembered being bounced hard across the deck, only to have the sea lift him before plunging him deep into the brine. After a lifetime thrashing in the dark waters, he'd finally sputtered to the surface. All he'd heard then was the howling shriek of the wind before another crashing wall of water drove him under again. Somehow he'd survived it all, though he had no idea how.

He stared again at a seal, who was watching him intently. For an insane moment, thoughts of legends told by sailors clouded his reason.

A gust of cold wind blasting mercilessly across the stormy water instantly sobered him. He was soaked through and chilled to the bone. Colin managed to push himself to his feet and climb out of the tidal pool.

Another image of dark eyes looking down at him flashed through his mind. The eyes of a young woman. He remembered more now. Someone pulling him through the water. Propping him on the rock. She had been no apparition. Colin braced himself against the wind and let his gaze sweep over his surroundings.

"WHERE ARE YOU?" He shouted over the wind. There was not a boat or person, not even a tree in sight, and the rising slope of rocky ground straight ahead hampered Colin's vision of what lay beyond.

"And where am I?" he muttered to himself.

The Macpherson ship had been too far north for him to wash ashore on English soil. The storm could not have driven them as far east as the continent. This had to be Scotland.

Colin knew he could die of the cold once night fell. He had to determine his whereabouts and find a protected place to wait out the storm.

He looked around again at his surroundings. He couldn't shake the sensation that he was being watched, and he didn't think it was just the seals. There was no one else in sight, though. His hand reached for the dirk he always kept at his belt, but it was missing. He picked up a solid branch of driftwood and started up the rise.

His trek was slow, but the distance was short. Upon reaching the crest of the brae, he sat on a boulder jutting through the long grass. One look and he recognized the place.

Colin Macpherson had grown up sailing aboard ships. Standing on the stern deck beside his grandfather, his uncle, and lately his older brother, he'd covered this coast many times over the years. Colin was familiar with every port, every inlet, every island from the Shetlands to Dover in the east, and from Stornaway to Cornwall in the west. He'd sailed from Mull to France and back again a dozen times. And he knew the history of this Scottish coast as well as he knew his clan's name.

He was on the May, a small island east of the Firth of Forth. It was well known to sailors as a graveyard for errant ships. Many vessels, passing too close to the jagged rocks above and beneath the surface, had met their end along its western shore. And the sand bars to the east were just as deadly. A hill, the highest point, rose up almost at the center of the island. To the west sharp bluffs dropped off to the sea. To his right, he could see the sloping stretches of rock and sea grass that ended at the water. To his left, the low walls and the five or six ruined buildings of an abandoned priory.

Knowing where he was eased Colin's mind a great deal. He was safe here, and it was only matter of time before Alexander would turn his ship around and come looking for him.

The wind at his back cut through his wet clothing, and he shivered as he pushed on. It was said that the island had once been a destination for religious pilgrims, drawing many across the water year after year. The priory, built centuries ago, had been dedicated to a St. Adrian, who'd been murdered here by marauding Danes in the dark time.

As Colin made his way toward the buildings, he recalled hearing that the monks had deserted the island before his grandfather's time. Only an old man and his wife lived out here now, feeding the occasional pilgrims and lighting a large fire during storms to warn the ships off.

Colin didn't remember seeing any fire in his one glimpse of the island before being swept overboard. But he didn't believe the face he'd seen—a face already etched in his mind—had been very old, either.

He fought off the fatigue that was gathering around him like a fog, and approached the stone buildings of the old priory. To his right he saw a protected hollow where a small flock of sheep huddled together out of the wind. Ahead, he couldn't tell which of the decrepit buildings might have housed the couple.

"HULLO!" At his shout the animals shuffled about and bleated loudly. Colin wished he knew something more of the keeper and his wife—even a name would have been a good place to start. No one was showing themselves, and the gray stone buildings showed no sign of anyone living inside of them.

Crossing a moor of knee high grass, Colin found himself on a path, of sorts, that led past a little patch of land protected from the west wind by a grove of short, wind-stunted pines. The remains of what looked to be last year's gardens affirmed that the couple still lived on the island.

It wasn't until he was past the first line of buildings that he saw wisps of smoke being whipped from a recently built chimney above a squat, two-story building. As Colin grew near, his excitement grew at the tidy condition of the protected yard.

"Anyone here?" he called up the set of ancient stairs that lay beyond the door.

The lack of an answer didn't deter him. The wind was howling behind him. The steps had been recently swept. A large pile of gnarled driftwood was stacked neatly at the foot of the stairs. Colin drew in a deep breath and started up the stairs. Reaching the upper floor, he saw the glowing embers in the hearth at the end of the room.

Someone *had* to be around, but the fact that they weren't showing themselves didn't make him feel particularly comfortable.

"I intend no harm," he said loudly, eyeing the slabs of smoked fish and long, looping strands of shells hanging from the low rafters. His gaze swept every dark corner and crevice. The dim light coming in through the narrow slits in the walls added to the faint light from the hearth, but did little to help brighten the room. "I was swept off my ship in the storm."

He stepped cautiously into the room. A torn net—half mended—lay by a small, carefully stacked pile of bleached whale bones. Something crunched beneath his boots. He looked down. All around the room, seashells of every size and description could be seen, and a small hill of them sat on a sheepskin in the corner, beside a small loom.

The fire crackled and sparked in the hearth, drawing his attention again. He noticed the cauldron hanging over the fire. Someone's dinner. "I think someone...perhaps 'twas you...pulled me out."

One thing that he remembered hearing about the old couple that lived on the island was that they'd never been particularly hospitable. But they'd also not been afraid of the fishermen or sailors who ended up on their shores.

"My people will be back for me soon." He spoke louder this time, eyeing the ladder resting against a wall. Near it, a line of dark boards across the beams created a loft area above. "I need to borrow a blanket...maybe some food...and I'll repay you for it."

He climbed the ladder and peered into the darkness of the large open space above. The room appeared to be used for storage.

"Hullo." There was no one up here.

Colin climbed back down the ladder and looked out the narrow slit of a window at the sea. The storm was still blowing hard, and he could barely see past the shoreline. He could only imagine how upset Alexander would be right now. But there was no coming after him this night or in this weather.

Resigned to spend the night outside, Colin reached for a thick woolen blanket that sat on a shelf beside the hearth. As he picked it up, something that had been folded within the blanket fell onto the floor. He crouched and stared at a small bundle of mending at his feet. The intricate lace edging on a child's white cap caught his attention first. He touched the soft wool cloth of a dress. Perplexed, he frowned at a child's linen apron and again at the cap he'd seen first. He picked up the items one by one and looked at them intently, wondering why two old people would keep such things.

He looked about the room again. There was one wooden bowl near the hearth—one spoon. On the floor in one corner, there was a small bed of straw and blankets suitable for one person. He touched the dress again. The dark eyes of a woman looking down at him flashed through his mind again. Colin carefully wrapped the bundle of child's clothing in the blanket and put it back where he'd found it.

Pushing himself to his feet, he picked up a more worn woolen blanket that he saw folded by the bed and draped it over his shoulders.

With one more glance around, he descended the stairs and pushed out into the storm.

Added to the shivering that had taken control of Tess's limbs, her teeth were now chattering and she could not stop it. Her clothes were soaked through from her efforts to get the man out of the tidal pool. Her skin was clammy, and she was feeling chilled to the bone. The leather cloak offered some protection against the bitter wind-driven rain, but her body seemed unable to produce any warmth as she lay flat on her stomach on the rocks to the west of the priory.

Tess's eyes narrowed as the Highlander finally came out of her house.

She had hoped to go inside and get a blanket or two and some food before fleeing to the caves on the western side of the island. In fact, it was much more than a hope, she corrected. She *had* to get some supplies before retreating there. Who knew how long the storm surges would require her to stay hidden or how many days it would be before the Highlander's people would return?

Night was quickly dropping its dark cloak over the island. The storm, though, seemed to have shaken off its leash. It was now hammering the island with ten times the fury it had before. A freezing rain had been falling in fits and spurts. It was not a night to be out.

He was making a fire. She saw him walk back toward her house a couple of times. Each time he came back carrying armfuls of dry seaweed and driftwood she had diligently gathered, she felt herself growing angrier. And if this wasn't enough, he was building his fire within the area protected by the priory walls.

A standing stone wall served as a windbreak. The location kept away the rain. There he was, safe and warm. But there was also no chance of any passing ship seeing his fire.

And what was worse, he was building it where she could not possibly get inside her house without being seen by him.

She should have left him to swallow more seawater.

The sparking flames, hissing and crackling, climbed high into the night. Colin's clothes were practically dry now. His plaid, with the added layer from the blanket he'd borrowed from the house, was keeping the worst of the rain off him.

He was surprised to find that he was even growing hungry. He considered for a moment the food he'd seen in the priory building. Making one last trip, he entered and approached the hearth, picking up the wooden spoon beside the still-simmering cauldron. One mouthful of the thick, bitter-tasting brew, though, and his stomach wrenched. Colin ran outside, gulping down draughts of fresh salt air to keep his guts from spilling out.

His appetite was now gone, most likely for good, and he returned to the fire. Even as he walked, he could feel the eyes of someone watching him from the darkness. He settled by the wall for the night and thought about the old stories of seals who became women.

Tess started abruptly. She didn't know how long she had been lying on the cold rocks. It was still night, and the storm was continuing unabated. Her limbs were stiff and numb. The chattering of her teeth was like thunder rolling painfully through her head. At some point, she thought, she must have fallen sleep. But she wasn't sure.

Lifting her head off the rock required an effort that surprised her. She pushed the hood of the leather cloak back so she could see. The sleety rain continued to pelt her, but the Highlander's fire was still burning below. In the circle of light around it, she could see his sleeping form tucked snuggly against the wall. He must be quite comfortable with *her* blanket wrapped about him, she seethed.

She glanced at the door of her house and back again at the Highlander. The light from the fire didn't quite reach the entrance of the building. He seemed to have gone to sleep with his back to it, anyway.

Her first attempt at pushing herself to her feet was rejected by her stiff, half-frozen muscles, but her second effort was more successful. Carefully picking her way through the boulders, she descended, praying that her chattering teeth wouldn't alert him.

There were other things that she had to be concerned with besides the storm. Tess recalled Auld Charlotte's warnings about sailors and fishermen...about all men. With the exception of Garth, there was not a single male in existence that Tess could trust. The old woman had been blunt about it. And she'd continued to preach the lesson even on her deathbed.

...If the filthy dogs find a young and bonny thing like ye on this deserted island, they'll all be thinking the same thing, lassie. They'll knock each other down, racing to see which one of them can lay his hand on ye first. But do not let them touch ye, Tess. Ye fight them, child, ye hear? Better yet, go and hide and do not let any of them see ye in the first place.

Tess circled around, staying in the shadows and crouching as she moved along the low stone wall that surrounded the ruins of the priory. All the while, she kept an eye on the man's sleeping form as she considered what she needed to take.

The door creaked a little as she pushed it open. She looked back

13

toward the Highlander. He hadn't stirred.

As soon as she had closed the door behind her, she stood in the dark and took off the dripping cloak. Feeling for the familiar peg, she hung her cloak and turned toward the steps. After so many hours in the cold, her knees protested as she tried to climb the stairs, but she pushed herself on anyway.

Food. Dry clothes. Blankets. Flints. She wondered if the pile of seaweed and driftwood she'd gathered and stored in one of the caves a year ago would still be there. When she reached the landing, Tess saw there was some red glow left of the dying fire in the hearth. The cauldron was hanging where she'd left it.

There was nothing that Tess wanted to do more than dry and warm herself first. In her rush to get to the fire, though, she slipped and nearly fell on some seashells that the Highlander must have moved. Quickly regaining her balance, she made her way more cautiously across the room.

The heat from the embers felt heavenly after her hours in the bitter wet and cold. She crouched on the hearth and added some dried seaweed and a couple of small pieces of driftwood that were nearby. While she waited for the fire to kindle and come to life, she pressed her hands to the sides of the cauldron and almost sighed aloud with pleasure from its warmth.

"I shouldn't eat any of that, if I were you."

CHAPTER 2

The young woman sprang to her feet and whirled around with the quickness of a cat. Colin stared at his own dagger, drawn and ready in her hand.

"I believe that dirk belongs to me," he said calmly.

She waved the weapon at him in a motion that he understood meant that she wanted him to back away. He didn't want her any more frightened than she was, but he was as far away as he could get. Sitting in the dim light against the far wall, he had seen her enter, only to slip on some of the seashells that cluttered the room. She had been lucky to not crack her head.

"Why don't you put that weapon down." He leaned casually against the wall.

She raised her elbow a little, ready to strike, and took a step toward the stairs.

Colin tore his gaze away from the dagger and studied the rest of her. She was the same woman that he had seen by the tidal pool. The same dark eyes sparkled in the growing firelight. But her face was stained with streaks of dirt, and in the dim light of the room, all he could see was that she was young…well, younger than he was. Her dark hair was soaked and a loose braid lay on her back like a thick rope. The woolen dress that she had no doubt spun and woven and sewn herself was also dripping wet. She was a wee thing, all in all, and Colin knew he could overpower her if he really wanted to. But despite the show of toughness, she was shivering and pale. Colin frowned, knowing that because of him she'd been forced to stay outside.

"I had no intention of frightening you."

He raised both hands so she could see he was not armed. She continued to inch toward the steps. Colin could see that she wasn't too steady on her feet. He straightened from the wall. The continuing storm was whistling in through the slits of the windows.

"Listen, you rescued me yourself. You know I was washed ashore. Alone." He kept his tone gentle. "You'll surely catch your death in this weather, dressed in those wet clothes."

Her foot went out from beneath her as she slipped again on the same damn shells, and Colin closed the distance between them. Before he could lend a hand to her, though, she rolled to her side and slashed at him with the dirk.

"Bloody hell," he cursed, glancing down at the torn sleeve of his shirt where the dagger had sliced through. His tone reflected his rising temper. She'd barely missed cutting his flesh. "I told you I mean no harm."

She was struggling to her feet, but he was through trying to help her. Taking one quick step, Colin kicked the dagger out of her hand. The weapon clattered loudly against the stone wall.

"But you cannot expect me to take it kindly when someone steals my dirk and uses it against me." He grabbed the back of her dress and yanked her slight frame to her feet. She was as light and helpless as a rag doll. He turned her around in his arm, so he could take a better look at her face. She hadn't spoken a word. Maybe she didn't understand what he was saying. "Now let's start from the beginning, lass."

She kicked him hard on the shin.

"By the devil!" He tightened his grip on her shoulder. "I told you..."

She delivered a glancing jab to his face and tried to push away from him. Angry now, he twisted one of her arms behind her and pulled her roughly against his body. The dark eyes were spitting fire at him, and she looked like she'd bite him if she got the chance.

"Now listen, I don't know what has you so..."

Her knee connected solidly and viciously with his groin area. He gasped for breath, and his hands released her.

As Colin tried to catch his breath, he saw her run down the steps and heard the door bang open. Suddenly, he'd lost all interest in going after her. She was a witch, a devil, a madwoman.

Nonetheless, she had managed to drag him out of the water, and he felt a pang of guilt.

Grimacing with pain, he forced himself upright and took a step. Limping down the stairs, he spotted the leather cloak that still hung on a peg. This was the same one she had been wearing when he'd first seen her. He stepped outside. His fire was starting to burn lower. The bundle of blankets and sticks he'd used to fool her were still against the wall. The storm continued to lash at the island, and he braced himself against the wind. Colin let his gaze roam over the ruined buildings and the hills around him. To his left, he saw a dark shadow move quickly over the crest of a hill.

"WAIT!" He set out after her. The fool! He was certain that there were no more buildings on the island. Cold and wet as she already was and without any kind of shelter, she would surely catch her death staying the night out in this weather.

Reaching the top of the hill where he'd seen her last, he stared in frustration at the wild and dark terrain around him. The sound of the storm was matched only by the loud crashing of the surf in the distance. The sleet was stinging his face and he could see very little. He had no idea where she had disappeared to.

"By St. Andrew, I told you I meant no harm," he shouted into the night.

Still, he was not ready to give up, even though he couldn't see much beyond his next step. The ground was shiny from the rain. Jumping down from a ledge of a stone, Colin pushed on.

She had to be a daughter to the reclusive husband and wife he'd heard about. But he recalled hearing that they were so old, and she was so young. And then there was the mending he found in the room—the young child's dress and cap. His curiosity was definitely piqued.

He had no fear of getting lost. He could see the light of his fire reflecting on the walls of the priory buildings. What he needed to be careful of, though, were the bluffs to the west. One missed step there, and he'd drop forty feet into the surf and the rocks.

And something told him his bonny hostess would probably not pull him out again.

Colin stumbled on a mound of stone and shells. Coming to an abrupt stop, he peered down. Right before him, there were actually two mounds, side by side. Crouching before them, he could see a carefully arranged blanket of shells with large smooth stones piled on top.

Graves. Two of them.

Well, at least he knew where the old couple had ended up.

As Tess worked her way out along the cliff, the wind buffeting off the rocks nearly knocked her from the narrow ledge a half dozen times. Once, inching across a particularly narrow ledge, her foot slipped on an icy spot. Tess clawed desperately at the slippery rocks, managing somehow to stop herself from falling into the frothy sea. A few moments later she had made it to her destination, only to realize it was all for naught.

The tide was too high. She'd never seen the water up so far on the cliff face. The waves were crashing in above the opening to her cave. The footpath on the side of the opening was completely submerged. It was no good. She couldn't get in.

If she had been able to get inside, she knew the honeycomb of caves well. Inside, some of the underground passages climbed upward. Even at the highest surges, there were dry places where she could take shelter. She'd be safe.

Desperate to get out of harm's way, she considered jumping in the sea and trying to swim in. On many of the lower caves, she'd seen the seals forever playing their games and riding the surf into the caverns.

Tess turned and started clambering back up the rocks the way she came. She was thankful that her miserable physical condition had not affected her state of mind. Banging her head against the rocks or having her body drawn out to sea by the tide was no solution to her predicament. Fighting with the Highlander had given her a temporary surge of strength, but as she finally climbed up over the ledge, she knew she had nothing more left.

He'd said he meant no harm. But Charlotte had warned her about the lies, too.

He was bigger. He was stronger. He was quicker.

He was a Highlander.

That alone gave Tess reason enough to distrust him.

Exhausted, she was barely able to lower herself into a cleft between two rocks. She was still exposed to the sleet and the rain, but at least she was protected from the wind.

Colin waited for the first light of dawn to lighten the sky before going out searching for her again. Other than finding the graves, no good had come out of his last attempt. But this time he was determined to find and bring her back. It had been damn cold last night. Hopefully, she was still alive.

The sleeting rain had stopped, but charred gray clouds continued to lock out the sky. The wind, though, seemed to have picked up even more.

Colin started out in the same direction he'd seen her go the night before. From there, he descended into a valley that cut the island in half and climbed the next hill. It was the highest point in the island. Standing on top of it, he now had an unobstructed view of everything, including the two piles of rock at either end, known as North Ness and South Ness. His eyes scanned the turbulent sea to the horizon in every direction.

There was no sign of a ship anywhere.

The Isle of May was much longer than it was wide. And he had been right the night before. There were no other buildings. Very few trees even. No place where a stubborn woman could have taken shelter for the night. But she had to be somewhere.

Colin tried to imagine what he would do in her place. The answer was simple. He would have stayed put and heard the stranger out.

Women!

He again focused his thoughts on where she could possibly have gone. The east shore consisted of stony slopes descending gradually to the sea's edge. A tidal pool here and there hardly offered any place to hide and not much in the way of shelter. The west shore, on the other hand, offered a possibility. He turned his steps in that direction.

Colin's hopes rose when he reached the high, rugged cliffs with their sharp ledges and deep crevices. Peering over the top, he gazed down the rock face and watched the many sea birds sailing along the line of cliffs, wheeling and sometimes landing on the ledges. They sometimes would disappear from his view. If they were nesting here, he guessed that there could be any number of caves in these rocks.

He could only hope that she had found some place protected from the sleet and the cold during the night.

He started moving northward along the cliffs, looking for a place to climb down safely.

Moments later, Colin saw amid the distant rocks strands of dark hair whipping wildly in the wind. He hurried to her.

She was lying curled up tightly in a shallow cleft between two rocks. For a moment, he thought she might be dead. He knelt beside her, pushed her long hair to the side, and touched the side of her throat. Her skin was icy cold, but he could feel a faint pulse. He pulled her out of the hole and rolled her into his arms. She mumbled something unintelligible and tried to push him away.

"I'm taking you back to your house."

She made a feeble attempt to push away from him again, but she was clearly exhausted. She ceased her struggle and slumped limply against him. Lifting her in his arms, Colin pushed himself to his feet.

"But I am warning you, lass. No more attacking me with my own weapon. No kicking. No fighting. No more attempts to unman me." He started toward the priory. She was slightly built, but Colin hadn't forgotten the courage she'd shown in facing him last night. "And no running away, either."

She mumbled something again and tucked her hand inside his shirt. Her fingers were like ice.

"I don't know how long we are going to be together like this, but you'd better get used to having me around."

Stirring slightly, she wrapped her arms tightly around his neck and pressed her face to the exposed skin of his neck. Her cheek was soft as cold silk.

"And I'll do my best…to get used to you, too," he finished hoarsely.

Tess tried to burrow deeper into the ground, but something was stopping her. The wind was stronger and colder. Something was pulling at her. She was so cold. She had to push herself in deeper to stay warm. It was right there, so near. She couldn't bear being separated from it, but she was being pulled away. She held on tighter.

"You need to let go, lass."

She shook her head. The words were spoken very close to her ear. It was a deep voice. It was the Highlander's voice. She tried to bury herself deeper beneath the stones. She had to hide from him.

"I cannot be much help with you wrapped around me like this."

Wrapped around me. Wrapped around me. She didn't know what he was talking about. She was wrapped around a piece of rock. She clutched more tightly. She was growing warmer. If she could just hold on tightly enough…

"Not that I'm complaining. But you're cold and wet and…and I suppose we need to get you out of these clothes before you come down with a fever."

Wrapped around me. The words were finally sinking in. She forced her eyes open and found herself looking at smooth muscles of a man's neck. She lifted her head off a broad shoulder and looked into eyes the color of a turbulent blue sea. His face was so close to hers. Hazy and confused, she studied every aspect of his chiseled face. At the same time, she became aware that her feet were not touching the ground. Her weight was being supported by pair of strong arms. An unfamiliar warmth seeped through her, and her gaze fell on his mouth. A hint of a smile tugged at the full lips.

"So, you've decided to come around."

"You…are *n-not*…g-getting me out of these c-c-clothes."

His expression turned sober. "I'm afraid you have left me no choice."

She started struggling in his arms. "L-let…me…g-go. Let…me…go!"

Immediately, he dropped her onto her bedding, extracting a sharp cry in return as she fell. She scowled up at him.

"You…didn't have…to drop me!" Separated from his warmth, she felt the chills again wash through her. The skin on her face was stiff. Her eyes felt puffy and dry. She tried to tug a blanket from beneath her and pull it over her, but her hands hardly responded. She could not move her fingers. She watched him move away from her to the hearth. Squatting, he started building up the fire. Helpless in the light of her useless limbs, she put her head down on the covering and pulled her knees to her chest. She was so tired. She felt like crying but fought back the impulse. "'Tis...c-cold in...h-here. 'Tis very...c-c-cold."

"You'll be warm soon."

The Highlander put another piece of wood on the fire. In a moment the flames were snapping and hissing, and he rose and came to her. He crouched down beside Tess and tucked the edges of the blanket around her legs. "I am glad that you at least understand what I am saying." His strong fingers started removing her roughly-made shoes. Tess was too weak to protest As he pulled them off, she realized she had no feeling in her toes.

"I am Colin Macpherson. Do you have a name?"

She stared at the pale skin of her feet as his large hands cupped them.

"We'll worry about your name later." He looked about the room. "We *need* to get you out of those wet clothes." He reached for another blanket that was lying at the foot of her bedding and tucked it around her bare feet. "Do you think you can manage it by yourself?"

She nodded weakly. But the loud chatter of her teeth was making it impossible for Tess to speak clearly. "D-d-dry...clothes."

"Where?" He looked about him again and then followed the direction of her gaze to the ladder and the opening above. She nodded when he pointed at it.

Leaving her, he crossed the room and climbed up through the hole to the area beneath the roof.

Staring dully at his legs as he disappeared into the eaves, Tess realized that she no longer feared him. The man didn't have to come after her. He didn't have to bring her back. But he had. She managed to undo the laces of her dress in the front. Her fingers were clumsy and her skin actually hurt as she peeled away the soaked layers and crawled under the blanket. She felt the intense weariness again weighing her down. And it was so cold. She just wanted to go to sleep and forget about everything.

Pulling her knees tightly against her chest, she closed her eyes.

Thin shafts of light from a number of breaks in the roof cut through the dim haze. Crouching beside the opening he had climbed through, Colin glanced about with bewilderment at the large open space. Yesterday, he had thought it was just a room used for storage when he'd peered in. Now it occurred to him that the loft was a veritable treasure trove…if one considered junk to be treasure.

But it was also the most organized midden he'd ever laid eyes on.

Colin couldn't stand up completely beneath the low, sloping roof, and as he moved carefully in the dim light, he ducked under ropes that had been strung from one end wall to the other.

Hundreds of castoff items, if not more, were stacked on the floor in orderly rows. A cracked flute. A rusted helmet of a design he'd never seen. A pilgrim's bottle that looked usable. A mortar without the pestle. Some kind of clan banner with all the colors bleached out. A rusted chain shirt. Most looked like things that might have been washed ashore from sinking ships.

Colin suddenly remembered the shivering young woman below and left his perusal of this room for another time.

Against one of the end walls, he spied neatly folded piles of what looked to be ancient, wool blankets beside a worn sea chest. A couple of moth-eaten woolen cloaks sat on the chest. Laying them aside, he pushed open the large chest and stared.

On top, an ornately wrought golden cross, encrusted with bright jewels, caught his attention. The piece was magnificent. He picked it up and looked at it. The cross hung from a short gold chain. The length of it was only suitable for a child. He remembered the pieces of mending he'd seen downstairs before. Carefully replacing the cross, he eyed a young girl's dainty shoes. Next to them lay two small combs. There were other items in the chest, but his thoughts were once again drawn to the wet lass in the room beneath him. He left everything as he'd found it and closed the chest.

Looking around, he spotted two woman's dresses hanging from a couple of pegs. Colin grabbed for one of them and started for the ladder before pausing. Going back, he took a few of the woolen blankets and one of the cloaks, too.

The fire had taken the worst of the chill off the chamber by the time he descended.

"I hope this will do. 'Twas no easy task finding it up there amid the…"

His words trailed off. Wet clothes had been cast off beside the bed, and the young woman seemed to be sound asleep. Colin was well aware of what too many hours in the cold could do to a person. He stocked the hearth with more driftwood and moved again to her side. He touched her forehead. She was still very cold, and her breathing struck him as shallow and labored.

"You can put this other dress on yourself…when you are ready." He spread the extra blankets on top of her and placed the dry dress within her reach.

Colin pushed the wet strands of hair out of her face and, for the first time, really looked at her. Dark long lashes lay peacefully against skin that had been gently kissed by the sun. He stared at the perfect symmetry of eyes that he remembered were so large and dark. She had a straight nose and full lips. With her thick, dark waves of hair flowing down over her shoulders, Colin could imagine she would look like a mermaid. She was young, but very beautiful, and he couldn't understand for the life of him what she was doing on this island.

Colin saw her shiver again. Gently, he touched the smooth skin of her face to make certain she was warming up. She rolled onto her side and clasped his hand between her own and laid her cheek on it. The simple gesture made him smile.

"I so wish I knew your name, lass."

"So c-c-cold…" she whispered weakly in her sleep, trying to tug his warm hand beneath the blanket.

He disengaged his hand from the young woman and instead tucked the covers more tightly around her.

"I am a man, my bonny islander, and there are limits to a man's restraint."

Her shivering was getting worse instead of better.

"'Twould be best for you to stop challenging all I say."

Shaking his head, he leaned over and pushed her closer to the wall. Then, with a deep sigh of resignation, Colin lay down on top of the blankets and nestled against her.

"I do not know if you'll get any heat from my body this way, but this is as much help as I'm willing to be." He crossed his arms over his chest and stared at the blackened ceiling above. "And not a word of this to the men who come back for me, understand? You're not to say anything about me lying beside you with you all…all naked beneath this blanket. And absolutely *nothing* about what a bloody gentleman I've been!"

She tucked her cold nose into the crook of his neck.

Colin rolled toward her and drew the bundled woman tightly to him, enveloping her in his warmth. "I have a reputation to protect. So none of this gets out. Do you hear me, lass?"

She didn't say anything in agreement, but she didn't contradict him, either.

A very good start, he thought.

CHAPTER 3

"He is alive. I know it," Alexander Macpherson said curtly to the two sailors preparing to take the news of his youngest brother's mishap overland to the family at Benmore Castle. "You tell them that."

The ship, still buffeted by the strong winds and stinging rain, strained at its anchor in Anstruther harbor on the Fife coast. They had been lucky when there had been a slight lull in the storm around midnight. Taking shelter in the barren, windswept harbor, Alexander had been striding across the deck all night, cursing the storm that was holding him hostage.

Just because his ship was trapped, though, the ship's master was not about to sit idle. Alexander had already sent off a dozen men on foot and horseback to the north and a dozen more to the south with directions to comb every beaches and inlets from Fife Ness to Kincraig. But the area being searched was only a small stretch compared to the shoreline south of the Firth of Forth, and he would need more men to broaden the search. He would find his brother.

As the two messengers dropped into the small boat that would take them to the shore and to waiting horses, one of the ship's mates spoke up to the small group gathered by the railing. "I for one have never seen a better swimmer than Master Colin."

Alexander understood the words were said as much for his sake as anyone else's.

"Aye," said another. "That sea could easily have carried 'im all the way to Leith."

"Knowing how ready the lad was to be done with that lot at St.

Andrews," an old tar added, "I'll wager he's swum all the way to Dundee. Why, the young devil's no doubt sitting in front of the fire at the Cock 'n' Crown right now, a cup o' ale in 'is hand and a lassie on 'is knee."

"Ye mean *both* knees." The other corrected. "The way the lassies throw themselves at the lad…" The sailor paused, shaking his head in wonder. "What young Master Colin says is right—why settle for one when ye can have 'em all?"

As the men laughed uneasily, Alexander looked out across the harbor at the storm-lashed sea. He wished he could be so sure. He wished he had Colin here now.

His ship's mate laid a hand on his shoulder. "We'll find him, m'lord. 'Tis a sailor's lot to end his days in the sea, but Master Colin's time was not up. I'm certain of it."

The ship's master silently cursed the storm in frustration. Though he'd continue to have his men scour the shore, it would be much easier to sail up and down the coast in search of him.

"While we're trapped on this barren harbor, I'm joining ashore to join the search to the south. Send someone after me if you get any news from the others."

"Aye, m'lord."

As Alexander called for a boat, he tried to push back the nagging voice in his head that kept telling him that perhaps he was not doing enough. But then, maybe all of this was for nothing. Perhaps Colin was indeed lost at sea.

Nay. He wasn't ready to deal with such a possibility. His brother had too much life in him…too much fight in him…to die like that.

Her first conscious thought was the realization that she was warm.

She snuggled into the familiar comfort of her bedding. Warm and dry. Tess let out a deep breath. She could hear the sound of the wind and rain against the walls, and the stormy sea in the distance. She'd get up in a moment and see about getting together something to eat. Aye, she was hungry and thirsty, and she needed to relieve herself. Just a moment more, she thought, stretching her muscles beneath the blanket, savoring the lovely warmth surrounding her. Her legs bumped against something hard.

Tess opened her eyes and froze, too stunned even to breathe. Inches from her face she could see the mouth and chin of the sleeping Highlander. The two were both lying together on the narrow bedding! On *her* bed! One of the man's lean, muscular arms rested on her bare shoulder. She had been using his other arm as a pillow. She could feel his warm breath caressing her forehead.

And she was naked, she realized with a hot flash of panic. She didn't have to lift the blankets to know she was bare to skin.

Tess moved her head only slightly to look down at his body. From what she could see, the Highlander was fully clothed and sleeping on top of the blanket.

Bits and pieces of a one way conversation rattled around in her mind. He seemed to talk quite a bit. She also remembered him being concerned about her. Aye, he'd come after her. He'd even carried her back here! And then she faintly recalled taking off her own wet, half-frozen clothing before falling sleep.

Falling sleep naked. Her entire body flushed hot at the thought.

She glanced again at him. But nothing had happened. He was fully clothed even now. Layers of blankets separated them.

Tess stared at the man's full lips. So near. A shadow of growth was already darkening his chin. His shoulders were wide. His strength was so potent even while sleeping. And still she found she was not at all afraid of him.

Tess instantly knew that spending too many hours in the cold must had done some serious damage to her mind. She had to somehow escape this bed and dress herself before the Highlander…

Her stomach growled loudly.

Tess held her breath as the man mumbled something in his sleep. Before she dared to move, his two arms wrapped around her like bands of steel, and he drew her tightly against him. Her head was tucked under his chin and her body was aligned perfectly with his.

As she was trying to think of some way to extricate herself from this situation, she was shocked to feel his hands move up and down over her back, as if he were trying to warm her. And it was working. Too well, in fact. In her entire life, Tess had never had anyone do such a thing to her, and a wild thrill raced through her at the feeling he was producing in her.

The thrill turned to real panic the instant she felt his hand stray a bit too low on her back. She was ready to awaken him with a jab, but then the Highlander rolled to his back and tucked her into the crook of his arm.

From this angle, she had a much better view of the room. The fire in the hearth had burned down to red coals. The wind was whistling through the small windows, and she knew the storm was still continuing unabated. The light was dim in the large room, and Tess guessed that night was approaching again. She spotted her wet clothing in a pile near the hearth. Next to the Highlander's other shoulder, she caught sight of a dry dress he must have brought down from the loft where Garth and Charlotte stored things. She'd slept there as a child.

Ever so slowly, she stretched her arm over his chest and tried to get hold of the dress. She couldn't reach it. Waiting another moment and making sure his breathing was even, she lifted her body slightly and tried again to reach over his wide chest for the clothing.

Getting hold of it this time, Tess gathered the woolen dress in her fist and slowly started to disentangle herself from him.

He released her, rolling slightly toward her. She sent a silent prayer of thanks heavenward when he didn't wake up. Pressing back against the stone wall, she sat up and—as the blanket fell away—wrestled the dress hurriedly over her head.

By the time Tess knelt up breathless on the bedding with the dress nearly covering her, she realized it was a miracle that the Highlander was continuing to sleep on like the dead.

After all the trouble she'd given him the day before, he certainly deserved *some* entertainment. Watching her struggle to put on the dress was all that and more, Colin thought. Her body was perfect, her skin smooth as polished ivory.

He made another mumbling sound, as if he were asleep, and turned onto his side.

Colin had been trying to imagine the different possibilities of how someone like her might have arrived on this island. From all accounts he could recall, the couple who lived here before were far too old to produce someone as young as this. So she was either brought here and abandoned, or she too had washed ashore. But when? And who was she? And who were her people?

He contemplated letting her know that he was awake, but the sight that moved before his half-closed eyes stopped him. She approached the hearth and quietly placed small pieces of driftwood on the fire.

Colin held his breath as she stood stretching the muscles in her back. Her long hair, an unbound mass of waves and ringlets, hung nearly to her waist. Flecks of gold reflected in her auburn locks from the firelight crackling to life beside her. She cast a hesitant glance in his direction, and he closed his eyes a little more.

A moment later, he opened them again and found her washing her face with water in a basin. From a leather pouch, she repeatedly filled a cup—a large shell, actually—and drank the water down. As she did, Colin's eyes were riveted to the smooth and beautifully shaped column of her neck.

Something about him drew her attention, for she lowered the cup and caught him watching her. Her entire body became tense.

"Good morning. Or is it the night?"

"Morning…nay, 'tis night falling." She quickly corrected herself while cautiously laying the cup aside.

He propped himself casually on one elbow, hopeful that she wouldn't feel threatened. "Did you sleep well?"

She gave a curt nod and glanced nervously toward the door.

"You were so cold, and I was truly concerned that you would have caught a chill or fever after spending so many hours outside." He sat up on the bedding. She took a nervous step toward the door.

"Please don't go."

Her wary look shifted to him. From the narrow windows, he could see that night had already spread its thick blanket across the island. The howl of the wind through the openings was indication enough that the brutal weather was continuing.

"I shall go, if you like," he said quietly. He straightened the blankets around him and started pulling on the boots that he'd taken off earlier in the day. They were still wet. "This is your house. You need not spend another night out in this storm."

She glanced at him, then at the door, and without another word she started for the door.

Colin was on his feet and had put himself in her path the next instant. "You do know that there is a storm still battering this island," he asked shortly.

She gave a small nod and tried to go around him. He blocked her path again.

"Don't you think I deserve an explanation?" He didn't give her a chance to answer. "By St. Andrew, I must tell you I am tired of these silly games you women enjoy playing."

"What games?" she asked in bewilderment.

"These games of pretense—of acting coy and hard to please." He held up an accusing finger before she could speak. "And don't give me that innocent look like you don't know what I am talking about. By now, you know perfectly well that I can be trusted. How many men do you think sail these waters who would not have taken advantage of this situation?"

"What does the behavior of sailors have to do with me going out?" She had a very expressive face, and it was showing her perplexity.

"What is your name?"

She successfully stepped around him. "I have to go."

"Wait. We need to talk about this. Considering everything, we can both stay the night here, warm and dry, like two civilized people." He managed to put an arm in the doorway to block her path again. "I shan't bother you…"

Obvious frustration creased her brow. "I have to go outside." She went under his arm.

"Wait!" As Colin turned to go after her, more shells crunched under the sole of his boots. He cursed the annoying clutter the woman lived with.

She was fast. He caught up to the stubborn creature again halfway down the dark stairs. Before he could grab her by the elbow, she turned sharply to him, her hands out to hold him off.

"Do not come after me," she snapped impatiently. "I told you, I have to go outside."

"But why? I have already offered…"

"Look, I was brought up with the understanding that there are some things people must do for themselves. Do I need to say any more?"

Suddenly, Colin felt like a complete idiot. "Ah. You could have explained this to me before…"

She shook her head and hurried down before he could finish what he was saying.

"You *are* coming back, aren't you?"

Colin noticed that in her rush she didn't even stop to grab her cloak from the bottom of the stairs before going out. He didn't move, though, wondering if this had been all a ruse and the headstrong woman was running across the island this very minute. Not that he would stop her forcibly if she was determined to go…er, hide. But it would be nice to know his honorable conduct was somehow appreciated. It wasn't too much to ask her to trust him until this storm was over, was it? He was still waging this silent argument with himself when the door opened, and she blew in amidst the wind and rain.

Her steps were much lighter. Her attitude much less tense. She climbed up couple of steps toward him but then stopped.

"I guess 'twould be better if we started all over again."

She continued to study him as if she was trying to make up her mind about whether it was really safe to come up the stairs, or not.

"My name is Colin Macpherson," he announced. "You found me yourself yesterday on the rocks."

He realized that her gaze was focused on the dirk that he had once again put back in its sheath at his belt. He understood her fear. She went down a step when his hand went to it.

"You can have this, if it makes you feel any better." Even in the darkness of the stairwell, he could see her watching his every movement as he took out the weapon and held the handle in her direction. "I will be appreciative though, if you promise to not use it on me."

29

Colin waited patiently while she studied him some more. "I will also be grateful if you decided to spare my clothes, as well. I know they are not in very fine shape, but they are all I have here and, considering the weather..."

Finally, she climbed up and hesitantly reached for the preferred weapon.

"Will I be safe?" he pressed in a lighter tone, hoping to ease her nervousness.

After she gave him a quick nod, Colin started backing up the steps. He couldn't understand it, but somehow winning her trust really mattered.

"I see you have a very interesting collection of *things* upstairs."

She tucked the weapon in a pocket of the dress and started climbing up, too.

"In case you are interested in adding my dirk to your miscellany..." As he backed into the large chamber, the sound of crunching shells drew a curse from his lips. "By the devil..."

"This is better." She was biting her lips to hide a smile.

"*What* is better?"

"Saying what you think and feel, instead of playing these games with words."

"Games with words?"

She shrugged. "I know what you were trying to do. But I am not afraid of you."

Colin extended his hand at her. "Then can I have my dagger back?"

"Nay, you cannot." She went around him and walked toward the fire.

He turned, managing to crush more shells. "Why, in the name of St. Andrew, MUST you keep these bloody...?"

"Colin Macpherson." She glanced over her shoulder at him and actually smiled. "A little restraint is good, too."

She was even more beautiful when she smiled, he thought. "Who are you?"

"Tess."

"Tess," he repeated, liking the sound of the name. Colin tried to pay attention to where he was stepping as he followed her. "Do you live here alone, Tess?"

"Nay...there are others." Despite her immediate answer, she couldn't hide the shade of color staining her cheeks. "My father...and my...my older brothers..."

He glanced about the room. As he'd noticed before, everything from the sparse furnishings to the few utensils indicated that only one person lived here.

"But they are on the mainland now," she blurted out, reading his thoughts. "They were out fishing when the storm swept in. I *assume* they must be on the mainland." She shrugged and moved toward the hearth. "They are very good water folk. They'll be worrying about me out here alone. Aye, I should think they'll be getting back anytime."

She was lying and Colin knew it. And she was nervous again. He'd seen the two recently dug graves last night. And he'd never heard any sailor speak of anyone other than the keeper and his wife living on this island. But, of course, there never had been any talk of Tess, either. He decided to let the subject rest...for now.

She was attempting to stir the contents of the cauldron. "Did I destroy your food last night by moving it from the fire?"

"This is not food."

"Then what is it?"

She pulled out the spoon and let the congealed mixture drop back into the pot. "Some of the sheep have foot rot...from the wet." She glanced at him over her shoulder. "You didn't try to eat this, did you?"

He swallowed hard. "Not successfully."

She smiled, and Colin was enchanted again. She hefted the cauldron aside and pushed herself to her feet. "So I assume you won't be hungry for awhile."

"I am starving."

"So am I." She pulled down a piece of smoked fish hanging from the beams overhead.

"Can I be any help to you?" The crunching sound of shells under his boots made him wince.

"Aye. You can stop crushing my shells with every step you take."

Colin glanced down at the hundreds of annoying items spread everywhere. He had managed to grind a good many of them into dust already. "Why do you need so many, and why can't you pile them all in one place, so they are not underfoot..."

"Why can't you watch where you step?"

He took the broom that she handed him. "I asked my question first."

"Aye, but this is *my* place. I can do as I wish. You asked to help. I am giving you a chance. Why don't you start?"

He planted his hands atop the handle of the broom and watched her move around the room, preparing their meal. "I thought you said you live here with your father and brothers."

"I do." She avoided looking at him.

"Then why did you say...*my* place?"

"I was speaking for all of us."

"How many brothers do you have Tess?"

31

"Two…three."

"And did your sister go with them too?"

"She did."

"But you didn't say anything about your sister before, Tess."

"You keep talking, and you shan't finish your job. And the way I was brought up, if you don't work, you don't eat."

"Tell me, Tess. Why is it that you haven't the accent of the folk who fish these waters?"

"That does it!" She turned sharply on him, a frown darkening her fair features. "You are going out this instant."

"Not so fast, lassie. You can see I'm working." With a smile, he started sweeping the broom across the floor. As she returned to her own tasks, Colin also started sweeping up undamaged seashells along with the shards of broken ones. He glanced up at her back. "I never thanked you properly for saving my life."

"Well, you might thank me by not getting rid of things that I value."

She hadn't turned, but she'd known what he was up to. "Are you sure you are not a faerie, lass?"

Tess turned slowly where she stood and shot him a mysterious look. "Perhaps I am. And perhaps you should leave off your talking and not rile my temper."

"I see." He contained the smile that was pulling at his lips. "And what will you do if I don't do as I am told?"

Tess scooped a spoonful of the hoof medicine out of the cauldron.

"I feed you this for your supper. Any more questions?"

CHAPTER 4

The dying fire in the hearth cast an amber glow over the chamber, sparking and crackling from time to time as a knot of brine-soaked driftwood crumbled into the embers. Sheets of wind-driven rain battered the stout walls, and crystalline mists drifted into the room though the narrow windows. Sometimes, a gust of wind would chase the acrid smelling smoke back down through the chimney, but Tess—lying contently on her bedding—was oblivious to all but the Highlander as he slept across the room.

Until tonight, she hadn't realized how much she missed the company of another human being. She had her animals, her gardens, her weaving, her fishing...all the tasks of living that needed to be done if one were to survive alone on an island. She had her shell collecting to keep her busy, as well. She had only occasionally thought about having no one to talk to, but now she realized that she missed hearing another human voice. And even more than that, Tess realized that even when Auld Charlotte and Garth were alive, she'd never known what it felt like to have a companion who was interested in her, who challenged her... and who tested her patience every other minute.

And, to be truthful, she loved the feeling.

Garth and Charlotte had been patient and kind, but very quiet compared to this stranger. They rarely spoke to each other, and for the most part, they would only speak to her to instruct. And though they had genuinely cared for her, Tess had always felt a barrier. Once, while she was helping Garth clean some fish they'd caught in their nets, he'd looked out across the water. A great ship with billowing white sails was moving southward. Without looking at her, Garth said that one day a ship would come and take her away from them. He'd said nothing else—and it had never come to be—but she'd realized that day that they were protecting themselves and their feelings. They knew they could

33

lose her at any time.

Tess could only remember bits and pieces of her lost family, but what she could recall she had never revealed. She knew Charlotte and Garth always assumed that most of her family had died in the same shipwreck that had placed her on their island. But the knowledge that there might be others who wanted her back had made the couple hide her away any time a fishermen or sailors or pilgrims appeared on the rocky shore.

She knew she had been a welcome addition in their lives. To be sure, they had been a godsend for her. And she missed them.

The Highlander made a noise in his sleep. Tess sat up and watched him across the way. Restless. Tonight, the two of them had argued more than they'd talked during their meal of smoked fish and dried bannock bread. He was so full of questions about who she was and who her parents were and what she was doing on this island. Tess had taken great enjoyment out of continually changing the topic and turning the questions back on himself. Naturally, he wouldn't answer anything unless she did. Alternately funny and angry, Colin had been entirely attentive to every word she said and every movement she made. So they had gone round and round, and she'd enjoyed every minute.

Tess tucked her knees against her chest and admired the glow of the fire reflecting off the handsome planes of his face. He was not like any of the sailors or pilgrims from the Highlands that she had spied on over the years. He was not loud or rude. And he had not tried to handle her with any of the roughness that Charlotte had warned her of.

As Tess considered him, Colin murmured something aloud in his sleep. She scrambled from her bedding and stood watching him move his head from side to side. He was struggling against something in his dream.

"STOP!"

She moved quickly to his side. He was still asleep, but his face was covered with sweat, and he continued to thrash about. His arms and legs were moving, too, as he struggled. Tess crouched down and placed a hand on his brow, wondering for a moment if he had caught a fever.

His blue eyes opened instantly. She immediately drew her hand back, but stayed where she was.

"I think…you were having a nightmare."

He blinked a few times, trying to clear his head.

"I *died* in my dream." His voice was raspy and hoarse. "I have never before died in my dreams."

The vulnerability in his voice tugged at her heart.

"Have no fear. You'll live a long and full life. The sea cast you up, so your life thread is that much stronger." She used the corner of the blanket and ran it gently over his brow and wiped his face. She brushed back his hair. He still had the dazed look of one who hovered halfway between sleep and waking. "That's what Charlotte used to tell me when I would have bad dreams."

When she started to pull her hand away, he reached up and caught it in his own. "Stay."

Her hand seemed so small wrapped in his large one. Tess stared at the contrast of their skins—at the strength that was so pronounced in his sinewy arms and yet the gentleness with which he held her.

"Tell me about the dream," she managed to say. "Sometimes it helps."

His eyes were so blue that Tess thought she could drown in them. "I had forgotten how to swim. My legs and arms were not mine to command. And every time I thought I could catch some air, another great wave would crash over me and take me deeper."

She edged closer to his side and sat on the bedding. Their hips were touching through the blanket, and she was very conscious of the contact.

"That is just a scare held over from your struggles during the storm." Her fingers moved of their own accord and touched the roughness on his chin. She touched the cleft and hesitantly traced his lips. The difference in texture was so interesting. "You are safe here."

Tess watched as his expression changed. Shocked by her own behavior, she guiltily withdrew her fingers. His eyes focused on her face in a way she could not identify.

"You said you had bad dreams," he said softly.

"Aye. Many times. Sometimes I still do."

"Were you ever caught in waves like that, too? Washed ashore?"

"I was." Tess knew she had made a mistake the moment the words left her mouth. She tried to pull away, but his grip on her one hand held her where she was.

"Tell me about it, Tess."

She shook her head and looked away. "There is nothing to tell. I...I almost drowned swimming off the western bluffs."

"You blush when you lie."

She turned sharply to him. "I blush when I am considering murder, too."

He had the nerve to laugh for a moment. She shivered as his thumb moved slowly back and forth across her palm.

"How old are you, Tess?"

"Seventy-one this month! Far too old for you to be looking at me like *that*." She pulled her hand free and practically ran across the room.

35

His laughter followed her as she crawled beneath the blankets. She tried to close her eyes and ears to his charm.

If the filthy dogs find a young and bonny thing like ye on this deserted island, they'll all be thinking the same thing, lassie... Charlotte's warnings were losing their bite. The fact that he was a Highlander wasn't even enough to worry her.

Tess pulled the blanket over her blushing face and tried to cool her blood. The problem lay not with the man who was watching her from across the room. The problem was with *her*. How had she become so stupid so quickly?

She knew she was in trouble if Colin Macpherson didn't leave soon.

Buffeted by the gusting wind, Colin stood at the very edge of the rock bluff and scanned the turbulent sea all around him. Not a ship or a boat for as far as he could see. He'd taken advantage of a break in the rain at dawn, leaving Tess to the sleep of the innocent. He wasn't surprised at the lack of any sails, though perhaps the easing of the rain was a sign that the storm was blowing itself out. Once the skies began to clear, he knew he would see at least one ship on the horizon.

More than looking for his brother's ship, though, Colin needed to get away from Tess. He'd desperately needed some fresh air to clear his head.

There was something about her. She was bewitching him. Young women had always been easy to come by. The Lord above...and his parents...had blessed him with a fair share of good looks. He had a good family name. He'd never needed to pursue any lass. And he'd never seen any need in settling down, either. The ones who'd come looking for marriage, he sent on their way. Colin's plans included no wife—that was certain! He had plans to sail the seas. Adventure, fame, fortune...those were the things he was after. And he'd never considered letting his plans be spoiled by one woman...in one port...in one bed.

Colin walked toward the chasm that cut diagonally across the island. Descending, he followed a freshwater spring and dropped down to a stony beach. The brown eyes of a half-dozen seals were watching him from the water. Spotting some driftwood that had washed in with the storm tide, he began collecting some to carry back.

He was the youngest son of Alec Macpherson, a Highland laird, and Fiona Drummond Macpherson. Through his mother, he was grandson to the great King James the Fourth and cousin by blood to the infant Queen Mary. Naturally, with lineage like that, there were certain expectations. Though he'd tried to fight it, his parents had insisted that he follow in his two older brother's footsteps and finish his education at St. Andrews. But now, by the devil, that was behind him. Now Colin was ready to follow his dreams.

From Ireland to Antwerp, Macpherson ships had been raiding merchant vessels from the continent and from England for at least five generations. As his grandfather used to say, the blood of piracy ran in Macpherson blood. Colin's youngest uncle, John Macpherson, had been the Lord of the King's Navy. His other uncle, Ambrose, a fierce warrior, had also sailed these waters and raided many ships before settling down to a life of service to the Crown.

Colin's older brother Alexander was master of the Macpherson ships now. James, the second son, had chosen to pursue—like their Uncle Ambrose—the life of a diplomat. This left a world of opportunity open for Colin, for he knew Alexander could only keep at this for so many years before his time came to assume the mantle of the next Macpherson laird. When that happened, Colin wanted to be sure he was ready to take charge of the clan's fleet of ships and continue the family tradition. Hell, the Spanish ships coming back from the New World were just bulging with silver and gold. They were plums waiting to be picked.

He simply couldn't allow any woman to interfere with plans like those. Even if she were beautiful and mysterious.

By the time Colin returned to the priory carrying a stack of driftwood, his mind was clear and his resolve set. No attachment. No attraction. No worrying about her, or even going after her again should she choose to hide. She had obviously been surviving perfectly well before his arrival. She would continue on just as well after he left.

Colin's resolve, though, only lasted until he came up the stairs and found her missing. Her bed was neatened. The fire was burning nicely. Some of her blankets were missing, though.

"Bloody hell!" he muttered to himself. "Don't tell me you've run off again?"

Colin dropped the load and went out, his resolve obliterated in an instant.

All he knew was that he had to find her.

Protected from the worst of the wind in the yard between the crumbling stone walls of the ruined church and the ancient cemetery, Tess moved quickly among the sheep. Beyond the low cemetery wall, a nanny goat stood watching the proceedings suspiciously.

From the first moment Tess had noticed the lameness in a few of the sheep and had discovered the cracks and abrasions between their toes, she had used the direct method that Garth always used to treat the flock. Move them to higher ground and spread the salve that he had taught her to make on the feet of any sheep that might be developing the condition. And after three weeks of it, she was happy to see that they were finally responding to the treatment.

The cutting drafts of wind that snaked into the yard were still cold, but the sky was brightening. Glancing up, she thought that the sun might even break through before long.

Kneeling among the sheep, Tess finished rubbing the salve on another of the animals' feet. As soon as the ewe was turned loose, she butted and pushed her way into a safe place amidst the rest of the flock.

Tess looked about her in search of her last patient. She found the pregnant ewe standing alone and watching her warily from the cemetery wall. "Come here, Makyn."

The ewe pawed the ground gently.

"You've been talking to the nanny goat, haven't you?"

Makyn looked away.

"Come here, good mother. This is the last time we'll be doing this." Tess spoke softly and took a small handful of oats from a pocket in her dress. When she held it out, the ewe still refused to look at her.

"Getting a wee bit of your own treatment, I see."

Tess felt her pulse quicken at the sound of the Highlander's voice, and she cursed her own treacherous heart. He was leaning over the cemetery wall and looking with interest at the potions at her feet.

"Well," he said with a glint in his eye. "From personal experience I can say that if she doesn't want anything to do with that poisonous brew, I don't blame her."

"She is just not feeling well today. Otherwise she would come." A breeze, riffling through his long hair, tugged at the ends of his tartan. The blue of his eyes this morning were a sure match for any summer sky. She tore her gaze away from his handsome face and stared at the ewe. "Come, Makyn."

The sheep edged a little down the wall toward Colin. Tess pushed herself to her feet.

"Stay where you are," Colin said. "I'll bring her to you."

"Do you know about tending sheep?"

"I've never had any interest in the silly creatures, to be honest. The women tend them where I come from." He jumped nimbly over the wall. "Never looked very difficult, though."

Tess bit her tongue and sat back on her heels. Just as she'd expected, as soon as he approached, Makyn scurried away.

"Hold there, ewe," he ordered. "I'm not the one with the poison potion."

Makyn bleated loudly and ran frantically toward the rest of the flock.

38

Colin rushed the animal, but his abrupt movements only served to rile the entire flock. In an instant, Makyn had blended in with the rest of the bleating, scurrying bundles of wool.

"Where the devil did she...? Ah, there you are, you bloody...."

Stifling a smile, Tess stood up and walked toward Colin. She put a hand on his arm, stopping him. "Not to be critical of your shepherding, but I shouldn't think Makyn is in any condition for this. The creature is probably only a day or two away from lambing. I think she's had enough excitement, don't you?"

His gaze fell on her hand resting on his bare arm. He had rolled up his shirt to the elbows. His skin was so warm, and Tess withdrew her fingers as if she'd been burned.

"Very well. I am your attentive pupil, mistress."

Tess didn't dare look up to meet his gaze. Instead, she focused her attention on the terrified ewe in the far end of the yard.

"Sheep must always be handled firmly, but calmly and gently, too" she said softly. "Running and exciting them will only invite trouble."

"I always thought the same could be said about handling people," he whispered in her ear. "I was firm, calm, and gentle when I met you, but *you* still ran away."

"That just shows you that I am much smarter than Makyn."

Tess tried to not be affected by his low rumble of laughter, by his warm breath caressing her ear.

"Makyn is still nervous. We need to approach her very slowly and quietly."

"Do they all have a name?"

"Only the animals that I decide to keep."

"Very insightful. The thought of having a 'David' skewered and roasting over the fire is not very appetizing."

"It could be worse."

"How?"

Tess moved away from him. "We could have a 'Colin' roasting over the fire."

"In that case, I feel much, much safer having a name."

"And another thing, you should remember that in approaching sheep, never look at them directly."

He was beside her again. "Very well."

Tess felt his hand take hold of hers. Stunned momentarily, she turned and looked at him.

His eyes were sparkling with mischief. "I thought it might be helpful for you to look at *me* as we approach her."

He was simply too handsome for her comfort. "And why should I want to do such a thing?"

He shrugged. His smile was warm enough to melt through a sea fog. "Perhaps because I enjoy looking at you."

"And why should *you* want to do such a thing?"

"You are beginning to ask far too many questions." He shook his head. "You might pick up my good habits...and not just the bad ones."

"You have good habits?"

"Some," he said softly, his blue eyes searching hers.

Tess's heart pounded wildly in her chest as she felt his gaze brush over her face. In sheer panic, she took a half step back.

"I...I think Makyn is calm enough now for...for us to tend to her."

Colin's eyes had turned a smoky blue—almost gray—and Tess felt her heart hammering in her chest. She wasn't sure what he intended to do, or what it was that she *wanted*. Stopping, though, seemed to be the best course.

He seemed to read her thoughts, and his friendly smile returned. "Very well. You lead and I'll follow...or just tell me what to do."

"I'll catch and hold her. You spread the salve on her feet. Or we can do it the other way around, if you like."

Of course, she could have done the whole thing by herself, but she suddenly didn't want him to go away.

"I don't think my stomach will allow me to get too close to that cauldron. Tell me what to do, and I'll catch her."

She took him by the elbow and brought him a little closer to Makyn. "Without looking at her, get a bit nearer. When she is within your reach, quickly reach out and grab the wool under her chin. Just tip the head upward. This will keep her off balance and easy to hold. Now if she turns her back to you, just grab her by the rear flank." She gave him a reassuring smile. "I'll bring the medicine to you."

As Tess went for the cauldron, she could hear the muttered curses erupt from the Highlander, followed by a loud complaint from Makyn. When she turned around, she almost laughed aloud at the sight of man and sheep tangled together on the ground by the wall.

"I don't know which of us is winning this battle," Colin muttered when she settled beside them. "But please make sure you put that foul faerie brew on the *sheep's* foot."

"Hmm...but 'tis so easy to mistake one for the other." She started rubbing the salve on Makyn's front hooves first. Teasing, she reached for one of his boots.

"If," he said sharply, "you want any of those precious shells of yours left intact, you won't even *think* about putting any of that on me."

"Do you mean the shells that you have already crushed by the hundreds?"

"There are a few left, I believe." He sat the ewe back on her hindquarters so Tess could tend the back feet. "Actually, there is something soothing about the soft crunching noise these shells make when I…"

His blue eyes widened as Tess held the salve up before his face.

"I am done with Makyn. You must be next."

CHAPTER 5

Though the storm's force had lessened somewhat, the wind continued to lash at the island. It wouldn't be long though, Colin thought darkly, before his brother's ship reappeared.

He worked alongside of Tess as she went about her chores, tending the animals, drawing water from the well inside the priory walls. She was capable and beautiful. Yet she was quick to discourage any advances he might make. Though he was not entirely surprised, given the lack of society here on the island, it was still somewhat disconcerting for him. To have a woman shy away from his touch was not something Colin was accustomed to.

Oddly, though, Tess's gentle rebuffs only managed to entice him more, for he knew it was not a coy game she was playing. She was as genuine as the sea was deep.

"Thank you for bringing this wood up from the strand."

Colin straightened after stacking the last of it inside the door. She had just come down the stairs. "'Tis enough, do you think?"

"So long as you don't start another fire in the yard as great as the first night. What a waste of wood!"

He smiled. "'Twas a grand trick to draw you out, wouldn't you say?"

"I shouldn't be bragging about that too much…considering you're still trapped on the May with me and no way off." She brushed past him and went outside.

'Trapped' wasn't the word he'd have used. If she only knew. Actually, he was beginning to think this arrangement was not bad, at all. Still smiling, Colin followed her into the yard.

"What's next?"

"Usually Garth would be turning over the garden about this time of year."

"How long ago did he die?"

"December. Little more than a fortnight after Charlotte." A deep blush immediately crept up her cheeks, and Colin saw Tess's gaze turn warily to him.

She had blundered again and told him more than she had meant to. If Garth and Charlotte were the old keepers, then Tess was totally alone. He turned away, looking absently at the ruined buildings that stood within the priory walls.

Concern for her slipped unexpectedly into his chest like the blade of a dagger. What was going to happen to her when the Macpherson ship came back for him? He frowned at the skies with the broken clouds scudding across occasional patches of blue. Determined not to press her for answers that she was obviously not ready to give, he turned back to her with a smile. Reaching out, he tucked a wind-whipped, silken lock of hair behind her delicate ear.

"Would you show me around the priory before the rain starts again?"

Tess gave a small nod and turned toward the ruined buildings surrounding them.

"Sailing past the island, you never get a feeling that this place is even livable."

"Is this what you do? Are you a sailor?"

"I suppose I am." If he wanted her to trust him enough to answer his questions, Colin knew he needed to set the precedent. "I have sailed on Macpherson ships for as long as I can remember. I have traveled from the Orkneys to Africa. But up to now, I've been more student than sailor." He glanced out at the stormy sea. "But now that I am finished at the university, I suppose you can say I'm a sailor."

Tess pulled the hood of her cloak up. The wind—wet and cold—was picking up. She started toward the building Colin guessed had been the original church. A long ago fire had taken the roof and the door was gone. Looking in, he could see a chancel with a stone altar at the far end. He could almost envision gray-robed monks chanting their prayers there. The end wall was half gone, as well, and several gray and white sea birds were perched on the bottom ledge of an arched stone opening that had once undoubtedly held a stained-glass window.

Her voice broke into his thoughts. "May I ask how old you are?"

"Twenty."

"You've accomplished so much already."

"Would you tell me how old *you* are?"

She paused first, but then answered. "Seventeen."

"Seeing how well you take care of yourself and everything around here, I should say *you* have accomplished quite a bit."

"'Tis hardly the same," she whispered.

He saw the flash of sadness in her eyes. "Why do you stay here?"

"This is my home…where I belong."

"But you were not born here." He held her gaze when she looked up at him, startled by his words. "Tess, I told you I have sailed these waters. For as long as I can recall, there was never any word of the old keeper and his wife having any children."

"I have been here a long time. If no one knew about me, that is because these good people were trying to protect me. They were afraid of what might happen to me if people knew I was here—the sailors of passing ships…or the fishermen from the mainland…or even the occasional pilgrims coming here during the warmer weather. Auld Charlotte and Garth wanted to keep me safe."

"I am not questioning what they did. What I am wondering is where you came from. Who is your family?"

She moved away from him without answering, and Colin followed, fighting back his frustration. At least she was no longer trying to feed him stories about her family being out fishing in storm-tossed seas. He caught up to her.

"With Garth and Charlotte gone, how will you stay here all by yourself? What if you should fall ill? or break an arm climbing the cliffs for birds eggs? or slip on one of those damned shells and crack your head open?"

She turned her back to him. He wasn't giving up, though, and moved around her. "What the keeper and his wife were concerned about before is nothing compared to what you should fear right now. You are a beautiful young woman, Tess. Do you have any idea of the dangers that…"

"Do you *want* to see this priory or *not*?"

Temper had moved in with the speed of a Highland storm, altering her mood immediately. Colin knew he needed to restrain himself from pressing on his argument until she understood her dilemma. At the same time, he understood her stubbornness…and her desire for independence.

He nodded resignedly, knowing full well that they were far from done with this argument. The wind seemed much stronger as Tess walked away from the cluster of buildings and led him to the middle of the old cemetery. Looking about him, beyond the walls, Colin couldn't help but be affected by the wildness and the beauty of the terrain—so much like the young woman who stood beside him.

"For such a small island, there are a lot of graves."

"Garth told me that more than one person is buried in many of the graves," she answered.

"How did he know?"

"In his years here he had to bury a number of pilgrims who died of their illnesses while visiting. He told me it was common to dig and find two, or three bodies buried in the small grave with only a layer of shell sand separating them." Tess stayed to the grassy path. "A few years back, I came upon some record books in the old chapter house. I believe the monks who lived here before left them. They are accounts of births and deaths on the Isle of May going back some three hundred years."

The rugged terrain seemed too uninhabitable. "'Tis hard to believe families actually lived here."

"I don't believe any families did live here," she answered, turning her back to the wind and facing him. "Not for any length of time, anyway. For all the years I looked back through in the books, there was only a record of one birth, and that was immediately followed by the woman's and the child's death. But there were many, many deaths. I think most of the pilgrims who came to visit St. Adrian's chapel and monastery were very ill. Some might have been cured and left here. But many died and were buried on the island. The accounts of it seem to have stopped, though, when the last of the monks was recalled to the mainland. Or perhaps he died, too, because no one took the books with them."

Tess continued to talk, but Colin's mind was focused on what she had said about reading the account books. *Reading.* Not many families in Scotland taught their daughters to read and write. The puzzle of her past continued to intrigue him. He doubted that Garth and Charlotte would have been able to read.

As a light rain started to fall, they headed back toward the huddle of ruined buildings.

"Does the Crown own the island now?"

"Nay, I remember Charlotte saying that St. Andrew's Cathedral Priory has held it for more than a century. Not that they are doing anything about it."

"But they were the ones who sent the husband and wife here, didn't they?"

"Aye." Instead of going back inside, she turned her steps toward the sheep.

Colin followed. "Don't you think they should be told that Garth and Charlotte have passed away?"

"I am doing everything that they were doing. The place is not getting any worse because of me." Tess searched among the sheep.

45

"I am not being critical of your abilities. What I am trying to say is that a big part of the keeper's job had to do with taking care of the pilgrims that come here in the better weather."

He watched Tess crouch before the ewe lying in the grass.

"What are you going to do when people arrive looking for food and shelter? You told me yourself that most of them are very ill. Now, how are you going to help them when you are hiding in some cave across the island?" He didn't give her a chance to answer. "And if you *were* to show your face and try to help them, how long do you think it will take before the news reaches the abbot at St. Andrew's?"

Her head was bent over the pregnant ewe. She pushed some oats toward the animal, but Makyn turned her head away. Tess didn't seem to have heard much of what Colin had been telling her. The rain was starting to fall harder again, and the wind was picking up. The hood of Tess's cloak was pushed back and her hair was gleaming from the rain. But despite it all, she was oblivious to everything but the animal before her.

Colin crouched beside her and pulled the hood over her hair. He saw the slight tremble of Tess's chin. "What is wrong with her?"

"I think she is ready to lamb."

"Now?"

"'Tis nature's way."

The sky overhead opened and buckets of rain started pouring down. "Isn't this something they do…on their own?"

She gave a hesitant nod but didn't move.

"How long before…before she is done?"

Tess shrugged. "It could be minutes, hours, or days."

"Well, you are not sitting here and holding her foot for days."

As if to contradict him, Tess settled more closely against the animal and draped her cloak over the ewe. In a moment, the rain had soaked her dress.

"If 'tis dying that you wish to inflict on yourself, then why not just walk to the west cliffs and jump into the sea."

"That would be committing a sin," she whispered absently, focusing on the sheep.

"Then why not let me walk over there with you, and *I* can push you over the edge."

"I already know that you won't do that." She gave him a smile that went right to his heart. "Colin, I cannot leave her here in the middle of this storm. Something is not right with her."

Colin considered pulling her to her feet and forcing her back to the priory house. It was so much easier to play the bully than to reason with a strong-willed woman. But her simple comment that she knew he wouldn't hurt her had touched him deeply. More than it should have.

Frustrated, he pushed himself to his feet and glanced around. "Would you be happy if she were settled in some dry place?"

Her dark eyes looked up at him hopefully.

"I can carry her to that wall where I settled in two nights ago. 'Tis fairly well sheltered. I can even make a fire for her, and bring in some seaweed and spread a dry bed." Mischief twinkled in his eyes. "I can even go up into your loft and bring down one of your wool dresses. Perhaps sing for her…"

"You are making fun of me." The droplets of rain shone like jewels on her face.

"I just needed to find out the extent of your attachment to this animal. I mean, you don't give a second thought to sleeping out in a freezing storm, but when it comes to…"

"Helping me to get her to that dry overhang will do."

Tess stretched her hand up, and he immediately took it, pulling her to her feet. Despite all the physical work she did on the island, he was amazed by the silky softness of her skin. He let go of her hand abruptly.

Makyn preferred walking to being carried by Colin, but her steps were slow and wobbly, her head hanging down. Tess ran ahead of them, and by the time Colin had led the ewe to the sheltered spot, Tess *had* spread a bed of dry seaweed for the animal.

"No fire," she said softly before he could make a comment. "And I *will* come inside, so long as you don't pester me about occasionally coming out to check on Makyn."

Colin controlled his urge to say anything, and instead simply nodded agreeably.

Makyn settled down on the bedding, but continued to show little interest in what was going on around her. The wind and rain were picking up in intensity. As time passed by, Colin could see that cold was having its effect on Tess. Crouching beside the sheep, she was beginning to shiver again.

"You promised to come inside."

Tess nodded and stood up. She must have risen too fast, for Colin saw her put out a hand to stop herself from falling forward. As he instinctively reached out to steady her, another instinct—that of pulling her into his arms and kissing her lips—suddenly blocked out all rational thoughts.

She was looking up at him, innocent and vulnerable, and then her eyes widened. As much as he wanted to kiss her now, he hesitated. Then the realization that taking advantage of her in this situation would be a mistake poured through his body like icy water. His hands immediately dropped to his sides. Without uttering another word, he turned and strode quickly away and across the moor toward the rocky cliffs overlooking the sea.

He had felt his body respond to women before, but there was something in his attraction to this island lass that was so different. He had never been faced with such aggravating thoughts of right and wrong. It was only a kiss he wanted. Only a kiss, he repeated to himself. So why was it, then, that confusion and guilt were churning about inside of him?

He reached the rocky bluffs and stared out at the rolling sea. Suddenly, the weather around him couldn't even compete with the turbulence of his mood.

When had wooing lasses become so blasted difficult?

CHAPTER 6

What was wrong with her?

One minute, Tess was startled by the intensity she could see in Colin's face. The next minute—as she watched him walk away—more than anything in the world she wanted his powerful arms around her again. She realized she actually *wanted* the fluttering in her stomach back.

All of the questions about living alone—questions that she'd allowed herself to ignore—were now rearing up defiantly before her. Even the sense of security that she'd created in her own mind had been shattered, swept away in two short days. And all she could feel now was a jagged and dangerous edge.

Colin Macpherson had upended her life, and now he had the nerve to walk out into the storm.

Tess went inside and changed into dry clothing. In a few minutes, she came out and looked at Makyn, who hadn't moved. There was no sign of Colin. Going in again, she spent some time in the loft area beneath the roof. Restless, she went down and sat by the fire, carding wool. But she could not sit for long and went out again. And then back in. And then out yet again. Still no sign of Colin.

She considered going after him—but then decided against it. As the daylight faded into dusk, the wind continued to blow, but without the sense of purpose it had earlier. Even the frothy sea seemed to be extending farther and farther to the horizon.

The thought of Colin going away without telling her...or saying goodbye...started as a cold white point in her head and grew steadily until it was a torment for her. There were no boats, however, left on the island. Not long after Garth died, his small currach had been battered to

49

splinters during a winter storm when the waves had crashed it against the rocks. It hadn't mattered to Tess at the time, and she was glad of it now. But that didn't mean other boats from the mainland were not already out on the sea. At any time, one could see Colin on the shoreline and carry him back with them. But if this was to be their fate—never to see each other again—then she was as helpless about it as she was about everything else in her life.

It was well after dark when she finally heard him coming up the steps. Checking the thick braid she'd made of her hair, she hurriedly tucked an unruly tendril behind her ear. She glanced down at her tattered dress and wished she had something better to change into. The excitement surging through Tess was unmatched by anything she remembered experiencing ever before.

Colin was wet through, and he looked extremely tired when he stalked into the firelit chamber.

To keep herself from going to him, she crouched before the hearth, lifted a cauldron onto the iron arm that extended out from the wall, and swung the pot over the fire.

"I thought perhaps you'd decided to take a chance on the sea," she said. "'Tis only a few leagues to the mainland. Not a bad swim, I shouldn't think."

Tess smiled over her shoulder at him and tried to pretend that nothing was amiss. He walked toward his bedding, and Tess ignored the crunch of the seashells beneath his boots.

"I cannot say I didn't consider it."

His admission stung a little, but she swallowed the knot of disappointment and turned her attention on the steaming broth. "It must be the food that is keeping you here, then."

"Nay! 'Tis these bloody shells. I'm growing quite fond of the things."

Tess glanced over her shoulder, but her retort caught in her throat. With his back to her, Colin was pulling his wet shirt over his head. He turned abruptly and caught her looking at him.

"I..." Tess knew her face was betraying the heat that had suddenly come over her. She looked quickly away and gestured to the ladder. "There is...I mean, Garth had a good shirt if you want a dry one."

"This blanket will do." His voice was low and hoarse, but she couldn't trust herself to look at him again.

"I made some broth. And there is more smoked fish. There is also some dried bread. It doesn't taste too bad with the broth, and—"

"Have you eaten?"

She nodded.

"You don't need to serve me, Tess. Why don't you go about doing what you usually do at night? I'll take care of myself."

As he came near the hearth, she moved skittishly across the chamber. She sat on her bedding and leaned back against the cold wall. Picking up a small sack of shells from the floor, she poured them out on her lap. She had already punched a hole in each carefully selected shell with an awl, and she now began stringing them onto a strand of leather. She watched him dip a bowl into the broth.

Colin had thrown a blanket over his shoulder. But she still managed to glimpse his bare chest every now and then. Tess felt delightfully wicked.

"So what do you do with all of these?"

She knew he was talking about the shells. "I make them into…things."

"What kinds of things?"

She shrugged. "Bonny things."

"Then why haven't I seen you wear them?"

Tess watched him pick up the bowl of broth and a chunk of dried bread and move back toward his bedding across the room. The blanket fell off one shoulder, but to her disappointment he caught it and pulled it back on.

"Because they are impractical to wear."

"If they're impractical, then why do you make them?"

"Because I like to collect them…and look at them." She pointed to the strands of shells hanging from the beams overhead. "And I like to collect them because I walk on the beach looking for things. And I look for things because you never know what treasure you might find."

"Or what trouble," he muttered, lowering himself onto his bed. He nearly sat down on the gift she'd left him. "What have we here?" He picked up the wooden flute.

"'Tis a cuisle, of course. I found it years ago washed up on the rocks." She saw him manage to juggle everything in his hand as he sat back and leaned against the wall, facing her.

"I can see that. Do you know how to play it?"

She shook her head. "Whenever I blow in it…there is this horrible noise that comes out of it. Neither Garth nor Charlotte could get it to play any music, either."

"But you've heard other people play it before?"

She hesitantly nodded. "I have these vague memories of a child sneaking out of her bedchamber and creeping down some ancient stairs to listen to traveling musicians. There was singing and dancing and…" Tess stopped abruptly, shocked that how real the images suddenly seemed.

She looked down at the pile of shells in her lap and tried to blink back the sudden tears that the memory triggered. But she had no past. For so long she had remembered so little of her life prior to the day that the sea had tossed her up onto these rocky shores.

"Would you like me to play this for you?"

Tess nodded and quickly dashed away a tear as he laid the food aside and brought the pipe to his lips.

After testing it a few times, Colin began to play a melody so hauntingly lonely and yet so soothing, too. It was a song that seemed so familiar to Tess, like it was a part of her. A part of her childhood, she thought. The notes filled the space between them. The air vibrated with the feeling Colin poured into the music. Tess saw him close his eyes. His fingers and lips and breaths seemed to be drawing out the very secrets of his heart.

She let the string of shells drop into her lap. In her mind's eye she could see a solitary tree, stunted and bent, braced against the wind. Beside it, she saw herself alone on this isle, trying desperately to remember his face, the feel of his touch…this melody…for the long time when he would be gone. Then, Tess also thought of *his* loneliness in being separated from the people that he loved.

When the song was finished, he played another, and another…and another after that. After playing for a while, he stopped and laid the instrument down.

As the notes faded, Tess dashed away a tear. "You play beautifully."

"This is an old and very special instrument."

"I want you to have it." When he started shaking his head, she pressed him. "You've given me the gift of hearing music again. Please!"

"Thank you. But is there anything I can do…well…?" His words trailed off.

Before I go, Tess thought, finishing his unspoken words. He *was* going, she reminded herself. Soon.

"You already have," she whispered, lowering her gaze to the shells lying in her lap.

The aching sadness gathering within her was growing more painful by the minute. She had lost people whom she cared for before. She'd had to learn to adjust and rely only on herself. But this time, with Colin, she knew she would feel something even more than anything she'd felt when Charlotte and Garth had passed on. They were old and it was their time. Tess knew deep inside of her that this loss would cut her very badly.

Colin finished his food and sat studying the flute. Tess leaned quietly against the wall and made the effort to string the shells that she no longer found so beautiful. Not long after, they both settled in early for the night, but sleep eluded Tess and minutes rolled into hours. She could hear the dying sounds of the winds outside. Gradually, the fire burned to embers and the chamber slipped into darkness.

Sometime during the night, when Colin's steady breathing indicated that he was asleep, Tess got up and went outside, throwing her cloak over her shoulders as she went out the door. For the first time in days, the wind had dropped off to an occasional sea breeze, and the cold seemed bearable. She raised her face to the sky and gulped a chest full of air. If she could only force down the painful knot of loneliness that she was feeling.

Makyn still had not birthed her lamb, which surprised Tess somewhat. The young woman was too restless, though, to sit beside the ewe. The scent of dawn was already in the air. She pushed herself to her feet and started walking toward the rocky shores.

The sea, the air, the sky…everything seemed calmer.

But not inside of her. Without the distraction of the wind and the storm, the reality of her situation on the Isle of May was suddenly pressing harder on Tess. In all her years here, she had never once considered the possibility of leaving the island. She'd never even thought of being forced to live somewhere else. The thought was frightening.

She still had the nightmares from time to time. The fleeting images of a terrified young girl running through dark corridors and passages. And there were other memories, too, that continued to haunt her. Faces that she could put no name to.

Eleven years had passed, and she had grown less and less eager to find the answers to her childhood questions. Charlotte and Garth had protected her and cared for her, and Tess had gradually become more than happy to forget the past. She'd never thought beyond just living the rest of her life right here.

She stood on the edge of a rock and let the cold water lap up to her shoes. Looking around her, Tess realized she was standing on the same rock that she'd dragged Colin onto not so many days ago. How had everything changed so quickly?

In a storm he'd come to the May. Like a storm he'd thrown her life and what she'd always thought she needed into total disarray. Restless and confused, she pushed a loose lock of hair behind her ear and braced herself against a gust of wind whipping off the gray-green sea.

Then, far to the north, she saw them riding the swells. Feeling a sense of panic rise in her chest, Tess strained her eyes to be sure.

Boats.

They were coming for him.

Colin woke with a start. He sat up, unsure for a moment if Tess had called his name or whether he'd dreamed it. He glanced immediately across the room. Her bed was empty.

She called him again. Her voice came from outside the prior's house. In an instant he was up and reaching for his shirt when she dashed into the chamber.

"They're coming!" she said breathlessly. She was a whirlwind of motion. Colin didn't think that she even knew that she had pulled his shirt down over his head and was adjusting his tartan on his shoulder. "Down the east side of the island. I saw them. We must make a fire… signal them so they know you're here."

Tess continued to speak hurriedly. Her fingers were flying as she attempted to help him finish dressing. But she never once looked up into his face.

"'Tis important where you set up…the fire. If you do it by the inlet, then 'tis an invitation for them to come ashore there. If 'tis on the high rock on the island, then you are only warning a ship of the dangers of the island reefs."

She continued on, but Colin was in no hurry. The morning light cast a soft blue tint across the chamber. Her cheeks were flushed. The smell of the sea and fresh salt air surrounded her like the most exotic of aromas.

"Come with me," he blurted out, surprising himself.

All her movements suddenly ceased. Dark, astounded eyes stared up at him.

"Aye. Come with me, Tess. I will take you to the Highlands. My family will welcome you. You'll like Benmore Castle…and you can stay there as long as you wish."

"Nay!" she whispered softly. "I cannot."

He tried to reach for her. "Tess—"

"Don't!" she said more firmly, taking a step back. "But you must go. Now. Please…now…Get them to take you to the mainland."

Colin paused. His mind raced with arguments, but she'd already heard all of them.

"And please don't tell them about me. Don't say anything about Garth and Charlotte being dead. Please."

He nodded, feeling no enthusiasm.

She reached down, picked up the flute, and put it in his hand. "Now go!"

She left him no choice. Frustrated. Angry. A chill of desperation settling in his belly, Colin strode out of the room and across the moor to the sea.

CHAPTER 7

*I*will take you to the Highlands. My family will welcome you…
Tess shook her head to clear the echo of Colin's words from her mind. They were *his* family. *His* people. She was nothing more than a stranger that he'd run into during a storm. He didn't need a complication like Tess in his life.

She walked as far as the ruined building of the chapel, watching him until he disappeared over the crest of hill. He never once looked back.

She stabbed away a tear. She could feel a sob rising into her throat and fought to choke it down.

Gone.

The urge to run away boiled up inside of her. The unfairness of what the rest of her life was to be was tearing at her gut. She thought of him standing by this ruined chapel, looking in. Tess could not take it any longer and turned to the western cliffs. Where could she go, though, to escape her thoughts of him?

Before she could take a step, however, Makyn's bleating penetrated Tess's distress.

She hurried to the animal. The pregnant ewe was still lying on the dried bedding. This was not the way the births normally went. If the ewe were not having difficulty with the lambing, she would have delivered by now. Tess immediately crouched beside Makyn and, pushing up her sleeves, tried to examine her for trouble. She had stood by many times as Makyn and the other ewes had given birth. For the most part, the sheep would simply lie down and birth a pair of lambs. Once and twice, though, she had watched Garth try to help a mother having difficulties.

Tess put a tight leash on her emotions and focused on the struggling ewe.

"Come on, mother. What is wrong?"

Makyn continued to cry out, but didn't move when Tess began checking her. It didn't take long to discover the cause of the sheep's trouble. She could feel the head, but there was only one leg of the lamb in the birth canal. The other leg must be stopping the birth from proceeding. And if Tess didn't do something, Makyn and the lamb could both die.

An instant of panic took hold of her, as suddenly she couldn't remember what to do. None of the births she'd witnessed had involved trouble like this. A complaints of the ewe penetrated her thoughts again, though, and she forced herself to focus on the laboring animal.

"We need to put this right, now, don't we?"

Tess tried to not think about the large amounts of mucus tinged pink with blood that were darkening the dried seaweed bedding. She forced herself to ignore Makyn's pained cries and futile struggles. Instead, she closed her eyes and, feeling with one hand, physically pushed the lamb back up the birth canal. It was hard going, but when there was space, she slipped her fingers around the shoulder, trying to find the missing leg.

Her fingers wrapped around the thin leg. Somehow, it must have caught on the rim of the ewe's pelvis. Working carefully, she started pulling it into the birth canal.

Her efforts had an immediate effect. As soon as the leg was free, Makyn took charge. Two feet appeared first. With the knees came the lamb's nose. She held her breath as Makyn paused before pushing again. And then the head and shoulders were out, with the rest of the lamb following.

Tears were coursing down Tess's face, and she sat back on her heels in awe as a second lamb slipped out with none of the trouble of the first one.

Makyn acted as if nothing were amiss and started cleaning both of her lambs. One of them was white and the other nearly black.

Her laughter mixed with her tears as Tess watched the new family. Animals were so much more resilient than people, she thought a few short moments later as the lambs tried to push themselves to their feet. The ewe stood up and shook herself before lying down again a few feet off.

"You're welcome," Tess whispered, letting out a breath of relief.

Clouds were racing overhead, though the wind was barely a breeze now. The morning sun was shining in its full glory. Thoughts of Colin pierced the moment, and she looked with a frown at the hill to the east. The weight in her chest returned instantly. Tess started to wipe away her tears, but she noticed her hands and arms and sleeve were a mess. She rose to her feet and found the front of her dress soaked and stained, too.

Tess turned to go inside and change, but stopped dead in her tracks
"And I thought you'd be spending the day pining over me leaving!"

Colin saw her blink once, twice, as if she couldn't really believe what
she was seeing. He pushed away from the wall of the old church and
took a step toward her.

"Well, is this the only welcome I get?"

"You...you're still here."

He cast a quick eye over her soiled dress and tearstained face. She
was a mess, to be sure. But a beautiful one.

"Why? Why didn't you go?"

"I decided the sea was still too rough." He came nearer. "And there
was the problem of not knowing who it might be that I was entrusting
my life with. And then the question of which village these fishermen
were going back to. And then the hardship of finding a way back to
Benmore Castle."

"Those are not very good reasons."

"Aye." He touched the flute at his belt. "The truth is, lass, no one had
ever complimented me on my musical talent before you. How could I
go?"

She smiled, but shook her head.

He halted only a breath away. Their clothes didn't touch, but he
could almost feel the heat emanating from her body. He reached out
and looped a finger around dancing tendrils of her hair. Tess's face was
lifted up to his.

"Why did you come back?" she pressed.

"I couldn't go, Tess. Not without you."

Fresh tears dropped onto her cheeks, and a world of hope shone in
the dark jewels of her eyes.

Colin glanced quickly toward the animals. "That was the most
amazing thing I've ever witnessed. How you helped her! I felt such...I
don't know how to say it! Nothing has ever made me feel the way I did
watching you. Watching them."

Her cheeks were flushed prettily. "I didn't do much. 'Twas Makyn's
doing. 'Twas only nature at work."

They both looked at the lambs, who were now nursing. Everything
seemed so perfectly normal.

"Well, those wee beasties are contented enough. You, on the other
hand, lass, are the one who needs some tending." Colin began leading
her toward the house. Stopping at the well, he drew a large bucket of
water.

"You should have gone with those fishermen. You've only made it

57

more difficult for both of us by staying," she said softly as they entered the house. "You belong out there. Among real people. Your *own* people. And I belong here."

"I don't believe you belong here, Tess. The people who cared for you are dead. The churchmen that own this island will think of you only as a nuisance."

This time she didn't argue. He put the water near the hearth and built up the fire until the room started losing some of its chill.

She finished washing her hands and face and reached for the dress hanging on a peg—the same one she had been wearing that first night. "Turn around."

"Let me help you, Tess."

"I'd do better to dress myself."

"I was talking about helping you with your past."

"Oh!"

"*And* the dress." He couldn't help himself.

She put her hands on his shoulders and physically turned him. He suppressed his smile and walked to the window. In the distance, Colin could see the white caps on the sea.

There had been more than the birthing of a pair of lambs that he'd witnessed outside. Watching her, he had seen her self-reliance and her readiness to act, but he'd also seen her frustration, her fears, and her unhappiness when she'd looked off in the direction that he'd gone. For an old hermit—or even a husband and wife—to choose this lonely life was one thing. It was not right for someone Tess's age—it was not right for Tess—to be all alone.

"Are we friends, Tess?" He had to ask.

"I...have never had a friend before you. So I suppose we are."

"Then do you trust me?" he asked without turning around. "Do you believe me when I say I genuinely care about your safety...about you as a ...a friend?"

"I do."

Her immediate answer gave Colin the confidence he needed. "Then why don't you tell me how you came to be living on Isle of May? And why is it that you are so determined to stay here?"

There was a long pause before she spoke. "I am needed here."

"Tess, this island does *not* need you." There was no sound of movement behind him, so Colin turned around. She had changed her dress and was standing beside the hearth, quietly braiding her hair. "I don't mean to belittle the feat you accomplished today or anything else that you do here. But for centuries these buildings have stood—such as they are—and for centuries more they will stand, too. What you cannot ignore, though, is the very real risk that you take living on this island *alone*."

She would not look up at him. Colin let his frustration show in his voice. "There are hundreds of ships that sail past here every year…more of them all the time. And there are many men who are…well, not so honorable as I am. Tess, you cannot even guess how low some of these men are, or how unspeakably they might behave if they were to find you here alone."

She turned her back to him.

Colin closed the distance between them and turned her around. "Give up this stubbornness. I plead with you as a friend to talk to me. To let me help you."

"I cannot go back with you to your people." Her dark eyes were determined.

"And why not?"

"Because…I am not helpless. I can take care of myself."

He fought the urge to shake her. "And *you* will. But you don't have to stay here to prove that. And no one would think you are helpless just because you come back with me."

She shrugged off his touch and backed away. "It has been so long," she murmured. "I don't even know how to live among people anymore."

"Garth and Charlotte were people. I'm people."

"You don't understand."

"Then make me understand."

She pressed her fingers to her temples and turned her back to him again.

"I am *not* giving up, Tess." He approached her again. This time he took her hand in his and held it until she turned to him. "Make me understand."

Silence hung in the room like the mists over Loch Ness. Colin didn't let go of her—but didn't speak either—as her struggles inside showed plainly on her face.

"We belong to *places*, Colin," she finally cried out. "You belong to…to Benmore Castle. I belong…"

"Don't start that again." The words spewed out more harshly than he'd intended. "People move to new places and fashion new lives for themselves all the time."

"But these people have someone they can go to…or travel with. They are *not* totally alone." She tugged her hand free and wrapped her arms tightly around her middle. "I have no one, Colin. *No one.* And I am dreadfully afraid of losing what I have here. As perilous as living on the

May seems to you, 'tis all I have."

She hastily moved to the ladder leading up to the loft area above. He watched in silence as she climbed the rungs and disappeared.

He turned and looked into the fire, fighting the urge to go after her.

By the devil, he'd only just finished at the university. Now was the time for him to live recklessly. To pursue his dreams of sailing the high seas. To live the life of a pirate. To take what he wanted. When he wanted. This was his time to have a hundred women in a hundred ports...without a whit of worry or regret.

At the same time, another voice argued, he had made a choice less than an hour ago not to leave this island when he'd had the opportunity. He'd chosen not to leave without Tess. By St. Andrew, *everything* was becoming too complicated.

Colin quickly realized that his own confusion was a separate battle — one that he would need to fight some other time. He climbed the ladder after her. Reaching the top, he found her sitting cross-legged beside the old sea chest — the same one he'd opened the last time he came up here. She had the top open, and she was touching something inside.

"This is where I might be able to help you," he said reassuringly. "Perhaps you are not as alone as you think! It may be that there are people out there who are kin to you. I mean, perhaps if you could at least tell me when it was that you came to Isle of May, then I can..."

"Six." Her attention was completely focused on something she was holding in her hand. "I was six years old."

Colin saw her lift a child's dress from the chest and lay it in her lap. He remembered the one he had found in a mending pile downstairs. She took out the cap next, then the shoes. And then he saw her take out the jeweled cross. She stared down at it.

"There was a shipwreck. I don't know if there were any other survivors. But I was the only one who washed ashore here on the May."

He came nearer and knelt down on the floor next to her. "Were your parents in the same shipwreck?"

"I wish I knew." She hastily stabbed at her tears. "There are so few things that I remember from before coming here. My name, my age — those I recall. Everything else, though, is hidden in a thick fog."

"But there are things that you do remember. Last night when I was playing music for you, the songs tickled something in your memory. You had heard that music before."

"Aye. Sometimes there are recollections that rush back to me. Faces that I cannot put a name to, or places that I cannot identify. Then there are other times when my mind brings a scene into life and I feel myself watching it. 'Tis like a dream, as if I'm on the outside of it, looking in.

But then it becomes a muddle again, and none of it makes any sense." Her voice quivered. "And then, there are the nightmares. There is one in particular that comes back over and over."

Colin held her hand tightly. "Can you tell me about it?"

He saw her chin tremble, and then she took a deep breath. "'Tis always night. There are loud noises, all around me...like people screaming. And I see a wee lass running scared. There are dark stains on her nightgown, on her hands and feet. She is clutching something in her hand. And there are footsteps behind her. Someone is about to catch her. And then she comes face to face with a wall of fire. There is no place else to go. And the footsteps are right behind her. I always wake up then. And my chest is pounding. And I am sobbing."

Tess's voice broke, and Colin pulled her against him. She came willingly. As she started crying softly against his chest, he found he had to swallow the knot that had formed in his throat.

"I'm sorry, Tess. I am very sorry. That wee lass had to be you." He pressed his lips against her hair. His hand caressed her back. The strong surge of protectiveness rushing through him was as unexpected as it was powerful. There had to be an attack on wherever it was that she lived. But for her to remember and reveal the painful memories made him realize how truly great her trust in him had become. "How did Garth and Charlotte find you?"

"Washed ashore in the same place where I found you. Unconscious."

"Wearing these?" He pointed to the child's clothing.

She nodded and pulled out of his embrace. "The things in this box are the only things I have left of that life." Tess clutched the cross in her fist and brought it to her chest.

"This cross must be what you are holding in your dream."

Her dark gaze met his. "Nay, 'twas something else. The nightmares are so real that I can almost feel it. I am holding a brooch in the palm of my hand."

A spark of hope ignited in his mind. With his thumb he wiped the tears from her ivory cheeks and looked into her face.

"Is there any way you can describe this brooch to me? Did you ever see it...in your dream, I mean?"

She nodded. "Aye, a few times in my dreams I've seen it. And then later..." She stopped and searched inside the old sea chest again. From the bottom, she slowly withdrew a flat object wrapped in leather.

Colin's gaze followed her hand's movements as she opened the packet.

"I didn't find this until a month ago, after Garth and Charlotte were both dead. They had it hidden up here at the bottom of the chest." In

61

her hand she held a brooch. Even in the dim light he could see the red stone set in the engraved silver. "This is the brooch I have been seeing in those dreams. 'Tis the same one the wee child has in her hand." She handed it to him.

On the brooch's broad sturdy pin, a swan rising from a coronet had been engraved. Colin read the motto on the circle of silver, and his breath caught in his chest. 'Endure Fort.' He recognized it. The words meant 'Endure with Strength.'

"I think…I think I might have been holding this or wearing it when I washed ashore. But what I don't understand is why those good people hid it away for all these years. They never said a word about it to me."

"Lindsay." Colin whispered. "This is the coat of arms of the clan Lindsay, in the Highlands of Angus."

"How do you know this?"

"Lindsay lands lie directly to the east of Macpherson holdings. They are near the coast, with only the land of the clans Farquharson and Gordon between us."

Colin thought back in time. There was something gnawing at the edge of his memory. Eleven years ago. He had been nine years old.

"It must have been about the same time that you disappeared that Sir Stephen Lindsay, the laird of Ravenie Castle, was killed in an attack."

He looked into her dark eyes, at her auburn hair. There were similarities, to be sure. Then, suddenly, the memories poured in. The stories he'd heard.

"Aye, on the same night and during the attack, his only daughter was whisked away by some of the laird's warriors and servants." Their gazes locked. "The lass was never seen again. Some thought she was killed, too. Others assumed she'd been hidden away for fear that those who had murdered the father would harm the child. The identity of the attackers was never discovered, I think."

Tess's eyes were wide. The teardrops shone on her skin. A look of disbelief continued to play across her features.

"But I believe there are many who are still hoping for the daughter's return." Colin cradled her face and looked into her eyes. "Like your mother, Tess."

CHAPTER 8

Tess was certain she had heard him wrong. "What did you say?"

"Lady Evelyn Lindsay, who was Evelyn Fleming before she married your father, survived that attack and the burning of the castle. I remember what happened now. Your mother is alive and well. She is living somewhere in the Lowlands—or the Borders—near her own family."

The sudden flash of hope was so unexpected that she didn't know how to react. "How...how do you know all of this?"

"Every Highlander knows what goes on with the other clans. Word travels on the wind there, and this was no wee bit of news. Besides, as I told you before, only the Farquharson and Gordon clans separate us from the Lindsays. We're practically neighbors."

"You are not just saying all of this to...to make me leave this island with you?"

"What do *you* think?"

His large and gentle hand was still cradling her face. Tess looked into the blue sea of Colin's eyes and had her answer.

"Nay, I think you wouldn't." The words tumbled out of her at the same time as she realized the significance of all she had just learned.

She knew her name. Who she was and where she had come from. Her mother was alive. She was not alone anymore. She didn't have to spend the rest of her life on this island, frightened and uncertain of what was to happen to her the next day.

The realization swept through her like a whirlwind, wreaking havoc with her emotions. She didn't know what to think first, what to do. Her mother was alive. She laughed, and then the tears began to fall.

Her father was dead. Tess didn't remember him, but she still had lost him in the same instant that she was told about him. Many questions battered away at her. The confusion of that night and what had she witnessed exactly that made her bury the memories so deep in the recesses of her mind.

"I am sorry Tess. I know this is a great deal to sort through."

"Nay, thank you." She wrapped her arms around him so tightly that there was not a breath of air left between them. "Thank you...thank you."

Tess was so lost in her own happiness and her own thoughts that it was some time before she noticed the difference in him. Colin continued to hold her, but she could feel the tenseness that had entered his body. Tess's anxiety again asserted itself. She pulled away.

"There is more that you are not telling me," she said, wiping at the wetness on her face

He shook his head. "This all happened so many years ago. I am just impatient with myself for not remembering more—remembering the details—of what was said about the people who supposedly had been behind the attack."

Tess placed a hand on his shoulder and pushed herself to her feet. The power of nightmares lay in how real they seemed. Perhaps, she thought, in how much reality was contained in them. If she were to look back closely enough, if she could force herself to remember the details of the dreams, then perhaps she could recall more of what she had witnessed as a child.

Right now, though, another problem was pressing—the person she had become. Tess looked down at her simple and tattered homespun dress, at her work roughened hands. The thought of what a noble lady named Lady Evelyn might think of the commoner who claimed to be her daughter was distressing.

He was reading her thoughts. "Tess, I know you must be anxious about being reunited with your mother again," he began, standing up. "But why not come back to Benmore Castle with me—just for a short time—until a message can be sent to your mother, and arrangements can be made for you to meet."

She had once before rejected this same invitation. Now, though, Tess found that she felt differently.

Eleven years was a long time. Whatever bond she once must have had with her mother suddenly seemed so fragile, especially considering how little she recalled. Still though, Tess wanted to go to her. Part of her did, anyway. But Colin had suddenly become the one person that she believed she could trust. He was her only friend, and a thought began to emerge in her mind.

"Aye. I will go with you to Benmore Castle. But when…when the message arrives from my mother, will you take me to her?"

"If you wish it."

Colin took her hand in his, entwining their fingers. He said nothing more, but Tess could see that he was struggling hard to voice something deep within him.

"You've no need to be doubting what we saw, m'lord," the burly fisherman growled at Alexander Macpherson. "Unless St. Adrian himself has taken to wearing a kilt and walking on the rocks, I say there was a Highlander on that island. And we've ne'er spied one of yours out there before."

"Did he call out to you? Motion for you to come ashore? Did he show *any* sign that he'd needed help?"

"Nay. Nothin' of the kind. The lad just stood there, a-watching the half-dozen fishing boats we had out. Then he just turned around and disappeared onto the island."

"And you didn't go ashore after him?"

"What for? No reason to." The man shrugged. "And we had fishing to do. After a storm like that, the fishing is always good. The rest of 'em are still out there, m'lord. I only came back, as I'd heard one of your men talking of it in the alehouse last night. He said there was gold in it for whoever helped find your brother. I'm thinking maybe I made a mistake coming here."

"Nay. You made no mistake."

The fisherman followed the Highlander out of his cabin door and waited as Alexander shouted orders to his ship's mate.

"He didn't look like he was in any trouble at all," the fisherman added when the ship's master was done. "And 'tis not like the lad's all alone there. Auld Garth and his wife have been living on that island forever and a day. I cannot say they're very fond of company, but the two are sure to give a man a meal or two and a dry place to sleep."

"Very well," Alexander drew a bag of gold from his belt and tossed it to the man. "I'll see to it that more of this comes your way if that the man you saw was my brother."

"Aye, m'lord. Wishing ye the best, I am." With a nimbleness that defied his burly physique, the fisherman scrambled over the side and into his currach.

It was too much to hope, the Highlander thought as he turned his thoughts from the man rowing toward the shore. But they had searched north and south along this coast for Colin and found nothing. With each passing hour, Alexander's hopes of finding his brother alive had lessened.

And then the fisherman had rowed his skin-covered boat into the harbor.

Perhaps St. Adrian wasn't finished with his miracles, after all.

It would be difficult to leave Tess with her kin, Colin realized as he moved quickly across the island.

There were other things that Colin remembered. Things that he could not tell her. Hints and accusations, whispers and rumors. Tales that might have been the absolute truth…or the embittered yearning of a clan that had lost its laird. Indeed, the Lindsay clan had seen no justice meted out to Sir Stephen's killers, whoever they were. Whatever Colin's recollections, though, he realized they were based on fragments of what a young lad had heard years ago from traveling merchants and musicians who had previously passed across the lands of clan Lindsay. None of it was worth mentioning to Tess now. Of that he was certain.

Within an hour, Colin built a large fire on the highest point on the island, and another one along the eastern bluffs. He had no doubt that Alexander would arrive soon, even without the aid of all these signs. But Colin had many questions about how Tess would react when the exact moment arrived to leave the island.

He frowned at the thought of how she'd sunk into a deep melancholy once she had made up her mind to go. Colin could understand her perfectly, though. This was the place where she had spent most of her life. These ruined buildings were home. She could be herself without worrying whether others would accept or reject her.

Colin had given her the privacy that she had sought. He'd come out to start the fires himself. But now, as the sky and the sea gradually became calmer, he could only imagine how her fears would be preying upon her.

He turned his steps back toward the building.

The outside, the stairs, even the large living chamber had been transformed in his absence. Everything had been cleaned and swept. Amazed, Colin looked at the shells sitting in a neat pile by the door.

As he was looking at the changes, Tess descended the stairs of the ladder. He saw the child's clothing and the cross and the brooch were the only things that she was carrying down. She looked self-consciously at her dress when she saw him in the room. He noticed that she had mended the holes. "I looked through everything that might have resembled a dress that Charlotte had put away up there, but there was nothing better than what I already had on."

"Tess, you look wonderful as you are."

She shook her head. "I know I don't remember much of that other life that I left behind, but I can guess at the importance of good manners and clothing and household skills—all those things that people deem necessary in a young woman who wants to make a good first impression. All of those things that I sadly lack." A blush had crept into her cheeks.

He immediately took her hands. "In what is truly important in life, you are better prepared than most women twice your age. And what you don't know you learn in no time at all. But none of that is important right now." He lifted her chin until she was looking into his eyes. "Just think of the thrill that finding you are alive will bring to your mother and your other kin. Think of that, Tess, and everything else will work out."

The uncertainties in her dark eyes continued to linger. "I...I don't want to disappoint her, Colin."

"You shan't," he said fervently. "You are alive, Tess. *Alive!* No mother would wish for a greater treasure."

She looked searchingly into his eyes, and he held her gaze for a long while. Then he smiled and glanced down at the things in her hand.

"Now, do you mean to tell me that out of an entire loft filled with baubles and keepsakes, that's *all* you are taking with you?"

Tess smiled at the small bundle. "These are the only things that are mine. The rest belong to this island. Whoever is sent to take care of it after I go should inherit them." She walked away from him and cast a sweeping look around the room. "There was one last thing that I was hoping to bring with me, though."

"If you want to bring Makyn and her wee lambs, it should be no problem."

She shook her head. "I wouldn't want to uproot them. They belong here, too. What I was hoping for...it doesn't really weigh much and doesn't take much space. But..."

"Anything." He would do anything to see that smile dance in her eyes.

"Those." She pointed to the pile of shells. "'Tis not really for me, but more for you, as I know how you've become accustomed to the sound of them crunching beneath your boots and..."

He smiled. She was going to survive this.

They both were.

The Isle of May was truly a place of miracles.

'Unparalleled' was the only word Alexander could think of to describe the thrill of relief that had coursed through him at the sight of his brother Colin standing on the shore of the rocky inlet. And the same word would have worked for his astonishment at the bonny caretaker of St. Adrian's shrine. But the ship's master had no way to describe his feelings upon learning that she was Theresa Catherine Lindsay!

Alexander had a far better recollection than his younger brother of the storm of rumors that had followed the attack on the Lindsay clan eleven years earlier and the young heir who had disappeared. He himself had been introduced to Sir Stephen Lindsay not long before that tragedy. He had watched the man fight in a tournament the king had held in the bowl-shaped rock amphitheater just outside the walls of Stirling Castle the summer before. He had heard stories from his own father, Alec Macpherson, about the Highlander's courage and his dedication to his king and his people. And as a child, Alexander had even overheard bits of talk of how beneficial it would be to both clans if someday Alexander were to wed a daughter of Ravenie Castle's laird. As it turned out, Lady Evelyn Lindsay had indeed borne a daughter.

But life's tragedies take no heed of men's plans. In one fateful night, the Lindsay laird had been killed and the bairn lost. Lost until now.

And Alexander couldn't stop staring at her. She was no longer a bairn.

Tess, wrapped in a stout leather cloak, was standing by the railing and listening intently to what one of the ship's mates was telling her about the sailing vessel that was at this minute plowing through the rolling billows northward.

"Could you possibly see fit to give *me* your attention for a moment?"

Alexander heard Colin's low growl, but answered without taking his eyes off the enchanting young woman.

"What is wrong, brother? Feeling ignored, are you?"

"Blast it, Alexander. If you don't look at me, I swear I'll throw you to the fish."

The edge in Colin's voice was not like him at all. With a show of reluctance, the ship's master drew his attention from the lass and glanced casually at the fierce young lion beside him. In looks and in size, he and Colin were very much the same. But in worldliness and good sense, Alexander knew he had more than a few years on his younger brother.

Still, though, there was something in Colin's look that caught Alexander's attention. It was either his tumble into the sea or his time on the island, but *something* had changed Colin. Or perhaps *someone*, he realized.

"I thought you were going below to change into a less ragged shirt."

"I went. I changed. I came back. But still you stand here looking like a beggar eyeing a free supper."

"Am I, brother?"

"Aye. The drool on your chin gives you away."

"You're probably right." Alexander gave a small shrug. "But see for yourself. The sea is finally smooth. A fair wind fills the sails. The course is set and all is well. I even have the dubious good fortune of being able to return my wee brother to Benmore Castle in one piece. But on top of all that, I have the bonny face of a young woman to gaze on right here on the deck of my ship. Why should I want to move?"

"To give her some rest from your lecherous looks! Can't you see the poor creature is nervous about all of this?"

"She looks quite well to m…"

"Never mind how she looks!" Colin snapped. "I'm telling you that Tess is plenty nervous about people looking at her…particularly pox-ridden, bow-legged old sea rovers like you. And since stepping on board, she's not had a minute's rest from your bloody staring."

"I don't know. She looks perfectly comfortable to me." Alexander smiled. "And I'll have you know, I am not pox-ridden. I'm as careful a man as a maid will find anywhere."

"I'm *so* relieved to hear it…you bloody goat," Colin retorted

Alexander slapped his younger brother on the back. "You, on the other hand, appear totally shaken." The ship's master lowered his voice. "Now tell me, you aren't already smitten by this lass, are you?"

"I'm telling you nothing. But I will say I was the first person to find her there since the old caretakers' deaths. Tess considers me…well, a friend."

"And I can certainly see that you have acted as a trusted friend should."

Colin was eyeing Alexander suspiciously, obviously unsure of whether the older brother was teasing him or not. Despite Colin's roguish reputation with women, it was already clear to Alexander that his brother's relationship with Tess was far different than any he'd been witness to before. There was a fierce protectiveness toward this young woman that was immediately obvious to everyone on board. Indeed, there had been no comments at all by the men regarding the days—and nights—that the two had spent alone on the Isle of May.

Tess's soft laughter at something that the ship's mate had said reached the two brothers' ears. Looking about him, Alexander realized that most of his men's attention was focused on her. From Colin's scowling face, it was obvious that he was seeing the same thing.

"You cannot blame them. The lass really is quite pleasing to look at," he said casually, wondering how long it would be before a brawl broke out. "And I'm thinking she doesn't even realize what a bonny creature she is…which make her all the more special, to my thinking."

As the ship dove into an extraordinarily deep trough between a pair of large waves, a shudder could be felt in the ship. Alexander watched as the ship's mate steadied the young woman by touching her elbow. The threat of murder on Colin's face almost made the older brother laugh, but he suppressed his mirth.

"Slow yourself down a wee bit," the older brother suggested placidly. "You've still a long road to travel before the lass is safely settled with her clan or with her mother, as Lady Evelyn chooses. You cannot allow yourself to get so riled over something as simple as who's looking at her, when there are far graver matters still ahead."

"Aye, and don't I know it! Tess thinks that the only challenge facing her is in getting ready to meet her mother. What she doesn't realize is that she should be more concerned with warding off the attentions of all the men that'll surely be pursuing her. I mean, she is not even considering the fact that as the heir to Ravenie Castle, she now has wealth to go with her blasted looks! Why, that alone will be drawing the wolves to her."

"Wolves, you say?" Alexander tried to hide his amusement.

"Aye…wolves," Colin repeated. "She is inexperienced in the ways of men, Alex. She knows nothing of men's lecherous nature. She could easily fall prey to the charms of any of them, and…"

"Did she fall prey to yours?"

Colin's head snapped at Alexander's direction. "Of course not. But I…I didn't pursue…and I…" He bristled. "'Twas a matter of honor!"

"Let me assure you," the older brother said confidently. "If she managed to survive Colin Macpherson's charm during your time together, then I should say she is well prepared to ward off any other wolves. In fact, with you acting as her guard dog, I shouldn't think any of us would dare to come within a league of the lass."

CHAPTER 9

*E*leven years had passed, but Tess discovered that she hadn't forgotten how to ride a horse.

Nonetheless, the long hours they spent on horseback the day they left the ship were a bit much. Having left the great sailing vessel in the narrow bay at the mouth of the Spey River, the dozen riders had worked their way down the winding river valley. On both sides, but more and more to the south as they rode, the gray green mountains of the Highlands rose jaggedly above them. The air was clear and cold, but by late afternoon, Tess was beginning to wonder if she would ever be able to walk again.

She knew it was her own fault that the Macpherson men had made so few stops. They asked often enough if she'd like to rest. Since she didn't complain or say she wanted to, they obviously were ones to take her at her word. And so they pressed on.

At one point, the valley—Speyside, Colin called it—stretched out like a long, broad trencher between round-topped gray mountains to the north and rising forestland of fragrant, red limbed pines to the south. The sparkling River Spey itself wound like a jeweled serpent along the wide floor of the valley. Tess's breath caught in her chest at the beauty of the scene. Farms and pastures adorned the hills and many crofters came out of their cottages—children and dogs around them—shouting their welcome to the passing riders.

As the sun kissed the western hills in its descent, Benmore Castle came into sight. At the crest of a hill, Colin touched her arm and pointed to the great castle perched atop a mound overlooking the river. Groves of tall pines rose on the north side of the edifice at some distance, and drawbridges crossed a number of ditches and moats that protectively encircled the high stone walls. To the left, a stone bridge spanned the river on seven arches. She gazed for a moment at the tidy village of wood and stone buildings that sat comfortably along to the south bank of the Spey.

A few moments later they rode through the arched entry and into Benmore Castle. Tess slowed her horse and fell behind the others.

Suddenly images rushed through her mind of another time. Another castle. Images of a child looking back from another arched entryway at night. Darts of flame shooting from windows. Men and women screaming and running in every direction. The girl crying and wanting to run back to the keep, but strong hands hold her back. Tess reined in her horse as she felt the grief rising in her chest.

"Are you coming?"

She blinked and saw Colin on his horse beside her. She looked down at his outstretched hand. She reached out and took it.

"I...I was back in time. For a moment, it felt like 'twas yesterday." She let out a shaky breath. "The visions. The nightmares. I was in another castle. And 'twas nothing like this one. There is peace here. There, chaos reigned and..." She became flustered, embarrassed even to have made the comparison.

"You are safe here, Tess."

"I know. I know. I am sorry, I shouldn't have—"

He shook his head. "After so many years away, 'tis only natural that a certain smell, a look, a shadow should bring back memories of what you once knew." His thumb softly caressed the back of her hand. "'Twill get better, Tess. Trust your heart and your judgment. You have the strength to see this through."

Colin's words of confidence touched her deeply. She took a deep breath and let his assurance flow over her. She trusted him as she had never trusted anyone.

"How did you become so wise at so young an age?" she asked.

"And is that all that you find interesting in me? My wisdom?"

Tess smiled shyly at the suggestive gleam in his blue eyes. She didn't try to fight the feelings that he brought out in her with a single word or a look or the mere touch of his hand. What was right and wrong was no longer muddled for her. She could no longer fight her attraction and her growing affection. She quickly realized, though, that there were others waiting for them. Blushing, she snatched her hand away and nudged her horse forward.

As they rode into the courtyard, Tess paused at the movement and the colors of men and women scurrying about to their tasks. The close was ringed with buildings huddled beneath the curtain walls. All around her people bustled about, obviously happy and safe and content.

Her gaze traveled upward. On the wall of a great building across the close, a large stone medallion displayed the Macpherson family crest. Her eyes were drawn to the lion at the top of the shield.

She stole a glance at Colin riding beside her and couldn't help but say her thoughts aloud. "I see the resemblance," she whispered. "Blond, blue eyes, majestic, untamed, fierce..."

"And hungry!" His low growl made Tess blush again as she quickly looked away.

To calm herself, Tess surveyed the entire interior of the castle courtyard. With its three towers, Benmore Castle was far more impressive than she could have imagined.

Colin was reading her face. "From the outside, it has the look of a fortress. But inside—you'll see for yourself—Benmore has many comforts."

Tess heard the pride in Colin's voice. She longed for that sense of belonging that had always been lacking in her own life.

Sitting astride her horse, though—here in the heart of the Highlands—Tess promised herself that it would not be like that anymore. She would face the nightmares. She would discover her past, and she would belong.

A group of people were gathered by a stone stairwell leading up to a large doorway. She saw Alexander already there, and a moment later Colin joined them, as well. A stunningly beautiful redheaded woman embraced him, and a tall, distinguished looking man with graying hair enveloped both Colin and the woman in his powerful arms.

"It does not matter how old, or tall, or broad we become, our parents have no reserve in showing their affection."

"'Tis a privilege to witness it." Tess looked down into the smiling face of the man who had spoken the words. He was standing beside her horse, ready to help her down.

"I am James Macpherson, mistress. Younger than Alexander by two years and older than that whelp Colin by four, but smarter than both of them and able to whip the two of them together." His smile was contagious.

"I am Theresa Catherine Lindsay." She had never said those words before, and the sound of them fell so strangely upon her own ears. It took great effort to say them without breaking into tears. She accepted the Highlander's help and dismounted. "Thank you."

"And you prefer to be called Tess. I know." He gently pulled her arm into the crook of his arm. "In fact, I don't believe there is much that I haven't been able to learn about you..."

73

She tried to gauge the seriousness of his words. James was taller than his brothers and very different in his looks. The second son's coloring was fairer than the other two. Even at this distance, Tess could see that he took after their mother. His long dark red hair, loosely tied, tumbled over his shoulders and down his back. His gray, piercing eyes sparkled with intelligence and wit.

"And how is it that you know so much about me when I have just arrived this moment? Or perhaps I should ask *why* it is that you should bother yourself."

"Alexander sent word ahead."

"Of course."

"And we learned that Colin was, unfortunately, still alive."

Tess stared at him.

"Aye. And though it might be too soon to tell you this—having just met—I fear I am duty bound to tell you what a mistake you made on the Isle of May in saving that pup's life."

She withdrew her hand from the man's arm and looked hard at him.

"I wanted to know more about you. I wished to know your motivation for fishing him out of the sea. Now, from the wee bits and pieces that I was able to learn, I surmised that you are selfless and have great courage. I myself judge these to be heroic qualities, and that brings us to your mistake in not allowing Colin to drown. You see, Tess, if heroic is what you were after, then you should have tried to save something worthwhile…a motherless seal pup, or a seabird with a broken wing. Instead, you have succeeded in ruining our delicately laid plans."

"Your plans?" she managed to get out.

He crossed his arms over his broad chest and gave her a curt nod. "Don't you realize that Alexander actually had Colin *thrown* overboard? And what a disappointment 'twas for all of us…"

Tess stifled her gasp and jumped back as a body suddenly struck James in the shoulder. The huge man only moved aside a couple of steps, though, and Tess was shocked to see Colin standing where his brother had been, taking her hand and scowling over his shoulder at the grinning James.

"My sincerest apologies for having left you alone with this chattering ape, Tess." He tucked her hand into the crook of his arm. "I hope he hasn't troubled you with his flapping tongue."

"Your timing, brother, is as bad as ever." James appeared on her other side and managed to tuck her free hand into *his* arm. "Tess and I were just discussing the merits of drowning you versus throwing you from the tower."

74

Colin ignored his brother and spoke directly to Tess. "The problem with the jug head beside you is that he can never forgive me for being so much younger...and yet so much smarter and better looking."

"My problem with you is that..."

"Will you two villains release this poor lass so she might be properly introduced to our parents?"

They all turned to Alexander, who was scowling fiercely at his two younger brothers. Tess instantly became aware of the watchful eyes and curious glances of the circle of people around them. She freed her hands from both men's arms.

"*I* will make the introduction," Colin asserted possessively, taking her hand again.

As the two walked side by side, Tess felt a weight drag her down with every step. She wanted so badly to make a good impression on Colin's parents. But all of her insecurities bubbled to the surface at once. She had already learned that Lady Fiona Macpherson was half sister to the late king himself. In her entire life, Tess would not meet anyone with nobler blood flowing in her veins. And she had already learned that the father, Alec Macpherson, was one of the most powerful of the great Highland lairds.

Tess's blood ran cold at the thought of how lacking she was in sophistication and charm. And how horrible she must look in the worn leather cloak that old Garth had left to her! She was just a plain and simple crofter who had lived most of her life on an isolated rock in the middle of the sea.

By the time they had reached the stairway, Tess's insides were as taut as knotted rawhide. Colin's mother was standing quietly beside her husband, the long red hair loosely braided and cascading down her back in glorious waves. Her gray eyes had the same shade as her second son's. The Macpherson laird was an older and more distinguished version of Alexander and Colin, but taller even than James.

"Welcome to Benmore Castle, Tess."

The laird's voice was deep and resonant. She extracted her arm from Colin's and curtsied politely.

"Thank you for having me here, m'lord...m'lady," she whispered softly, her head bowed. "I am dreadfully sorry to inconvenience you all in this way."

Lady Fiona reached out and took hold of Tess's chin, gently raising her face and smiling cordially.

"There is no need to apologize, child," she said softly. "We are delighted to have you here. We were so eager to meet you."

Far or near, Lady Fiona was the most striking woman Tess had ever laid eyes on. And then, looking into her face, she saw the warmth in those gray eyes and knew that all would be well between them.

"At last!" the laird said, drawing Tess's attention. "Finally I get a chance to thank this water faerie properly for saving our son's life!"

"I did no such thing, m'lord. I mean, 'tis not like that I *didn't* intend to save his life, but he was fine…well, without me. I just don't deserve any gratitude…."

"Nor blame either, I suppose?" At James's comment from the behind, everyone broke out in laughter.

"Smart woman, I'd say, not taking any responsibility for him." Alexander's comment drew another laugh from the men.

"Don't you pay any attention to them!" Lady Fiona scowled at the rowdy group around them.

"I shan't, m'lady. No amount of banter could hide the affection that exists between them."

Her comment drew howls of protest from the three men, but it obviously pleased the mother. Tess realized that sometime during this introduction, she had totally lost her nervousness.

Lady Fiona wrapped an affectionate arm around Tess's shoulder and turned her toward the door. "Why don't you come in with me and let the men have your things brought in."

Tess couldn't stop the blush from spreading on her face. "I am afraid I have nothing else. A woman doesn't need a very large wardrobe when she lives alone on an island."

Her hostess didn't seem bothered by this at all. "I understand completely, my dear. And I think I can be of some assistance to you with that."

Fiona Macpherson took the hand of the young woman and started up the stairway leading to the Great Hall.

Colin was beside her in a moment. "Would it be all right if I were to accompany you two?"

"Nay. You cannot." Lady Fiona said emphatically, waving him off and winking at Tess.

When Tess looked back, Colin was standing on the top step, looking amused. Behind him, though, the two older brothers were approaching. The laird appeared perfectly happy just looking on. As the two women entered the building, Tess heard a shout and then a cheer went up in the courtyard.

"Is Colin in trouble?"

"Always. I believe his brothers plan to use him as a battering ram."

"They won't hurt him?" Tess asked, concerned.

Lady Fiona gently patted Tess's hand and smiled. "Don't worry about him, my dear. He might be the youngest, but he has never had a problem holding his own. And whatever trouble Alexander and James cause him, 'tis only a fraction of what Colin usually serves them.'"

"But he's been away...at the university. What kind of trouble could he have caused from there?"

Lady Fiona lowered her voice to a confidential tone. "I have learned to not ask. Since these boys have become men, they fight about horses, tides, religion, politics, and harvests. And I am very sorry to say that every other argument seems to be about some young woman. I imagine, though, Alexander and James see your visit as a great opportunity to even the score with Colin for years of torment he's inflicted on them."

Tess didn't totally understand the meaning of what her hostess was implying. But she had a strong feeling that she might not want to know.

As the two women made their way through the throng of people inside the wide open doors of the Great Hall, Lady Fiona introduced Tess to an aging steward named Robert. The man's thin face creased in a smile as soon as he realized that there were no bags or trunks waiting to be moved upstairs.

"So much like you, m'lady."

"So much, indeed." Fiona Macpherson nodded good-naturedly, remembering her own arrival at the castle. "And forget about the arrangements we made before, Robert, I'd like Tess to stay in the Roundtower Room."

After the steward had hurried off away, Lady Fiona whispered confidentially in Tess's ear. "That is my favorite room. 'Tis the same one I stayed in the first time I set foot in Benmore Castle. I know you'll like it."

The rush of emotions came quick. Tess somehow managed to murmur her thanks. But no words were enough to describe how welcome Lady Macpherson had already made her feel.

"Never mind the builders milling about." The older woman waved to some men that were on their way out of the Hall, obviously finished for the day. "I believe 'tis Benmore Castle's destiny to be always undergoing of some kind of construction. My mother-in-law was determined to change and improve the place. And now, with our sons grown and starting their own lives, I am finding myself doing the same thing with my time."

"The Great Hall is truly magnificent." Tess let her eyes travel the length of the large chamber. Each of the plastered walls was covered with colorful tapestries and hangings of embroidered felt, velvet, silk, and damask. The floors were covered, as well, with ornate rugs, which shocked her. She'd never seen rugs on the floor before. These were fine enough for hanging. From behind them, the chatter of castle workers and warriors starting to file into the hall filled the air with laughter and good cheer.

Instead of going directly upstairs, Lady Fiona led Tess to the left, toward an arch, and into the quiet of a long corridor.

As the two made their way along, Tess asked her hostess about the history of the castle and the obvious improvements that had been made.

Fiona Macpherson was genuinely delighted at the interest and made a point of taking her through every room they passed. Tess was shown the latest improvements and those that had been gradually implemented throughout the castle over the past thirty years.

Lady Fiona's pride in the place she called home had no bounds. Tess saw the leaded glass windows, the new fireplaces in living quarters. She was led through the new kitchens and the brew house, and then up a level into some smaller guestrooms directly above. By the time they had worked their way around to the other end of the castle, she was amazed at the effort and obvious expense that had gone into the castle's renovation.

Casting a quick glance at the red-haired women, though, Tess couldn't help but speculate if her own mother was anything like Lady Fiona. She wondered, too, if the same kind of happiness would have filled Ravenie Castle if her father were still alive and Tess had never been taken away.

She had no answers.

Moments later, her hostess led Tess up a winding stairwell. The young woman held her breath as she entered the Roundtower Room that she was to inhabit during her stay at Benmore Castle.

"'Tis absolutely exquisite."

"I remember thinking the same thing," Fiona whispered, standing beside Tess in the doorway.

The room was large and airy, with leaded glass windows that kept out the cold, but still provided a sweeping view of the hills outside. The base of each window was corbelled with a bow-shaped oak sill wide enough to sit on. A fireplace had been prepared for an evening fire, and a large canopy bed with richly embroidered curtains sat against an inner wall. The floors were made of oak as well, and an ornate handmade rug covered only part of the burnished wood.

"I have kept everything the same." Fiona took hold of Tess's hand and drew her to the middle of the room. "'Tis delightful how much you and I have in common."

"Do we?" she replied, surprised.

Lady Fiona nodded, helping Tess out of the cloak and drawing her down beside her onto the bench near a small table.

"When I was a child, I was torn from my family, as well. Drummond Castle, where my mother and I lived, came under the attack the same night I was to meet my father for the first time. I left there, that night, knowing that I might never see…my parents again." Her voice wavered slightly, but Fiona's fingers was warm and steady as she held Tess's cold hand. "And like you I was raised simply, without the comforts and finery that life in a good family offers."

"But you were a king's daughter. I…"

"To those wonderful nuns who raised me, I was a castoff, no different than you were to the couple who raised you." She patted Tess's hand affectionately. "But I don't want to talk about myself right now. The only reason I brought up my own youth was for you to know that I understand what you are going through right now. I was the same way. And trust me when I tell you that it will pass."

Tess stared at their joined hands. "I…I *am* so nervous. There is so much that I don't remember or know. So much that I am lacking in my education, and manners, and in whatever 'tis that makes a young woman behave properly. I was delighted to hear that my mother is alive. But now I am terrified to think I should be a disappointment to her." Tess knew she was babbling, but she couldn't stop herself. "And we sent a message to her as soon as we came ashore. For all I know, she could arrive here any day, and I just know she will see right through me."

"Believe me when I say that I understand your concerns about seeing Lady Evelyn. But you should know right now that she will not be displeased with you as much as she is with us." Fiona touched Tess gently on the knee before she could voice an objection. "One thing no one has told you yet is that your mother has a deeply held prejudice against the people of the Highlands."

"But she married my father," Tess blurted out.

"Aye, an arranged marriage. But before that she was Evelyn Fleming, and she was brought up amongst her kin in the Borders area to the south of the Lowlands, almost to England, itself. They say her heart never left there. Many believe, for all the years that she lived at Ravenie Castle, she never really accepted her life with your father. To her, all Highlanders were barbarians, and she hated her time there."

Feelings of disappointment cut deep into Tess at this news. From Colin's chivalrous manners on Isle of May to the warm reception she had received from the rest of the Macphersons, these were warm and compassionate people. But even as these thoughts formed in her mind, another disturbing notion struck her. She was a Lindsay and a

Highlander, too. Did that mean that Lady Evelyn hated her, too?

"I've never met your mother, but your father was a good friend to my husband. The few times that I had the pleasure of meeting with Sir Stephen, I was quite taken with his pride in you." Lady Fiona squeezed Tess's hand gently. "And this is what you should remember, Tess. You look like him. You have his spirit. You should be proud of the strong person you are and your ability to survive as you have. 'Endure with strength' is your family motto, and you have lived up to those words. 'Tis quite obvious to me—if only from my three sons' response to you—that you are a pearl of great worth, Tess. Don't allow anyone to tell you otherwise."

CHAPTER 10

"Have I ever asked you two for anything before?" Alexander and James glanced at each other first before turning suspicious faces toward their youngest brother. The crowd of men around them laughed.

"Aye, you have," the eldest answered. He was sitting on Colin's legs. "You're forever asking."

"Every time you start losing, you beg like a bloody friar," James added. He was keeping Colin's arms and hands pinned to the dirt floor of the stable with great difficulty.

The two had carried him off to the stables as soon as their mother and their guest had disappeared into the Great Hall. A homecoming tradition since the boys' childhood, their wrestling matches had always been cheered on by the castle's inhabitants. They'd been the source of more than a few wagers over the years, as well.

With the older brothers firmly in control, the men started dispersing.

"Have I ever asked you two for a favor before?" Colin repeated.

The two Highlanders again glanced at each other before nodding in unison.

"'Twill not work, fox." James shook his head at the youngest brother. "After all the trouble you caused me when the Macgregor lassie was here at Michaelmas."

"And remember the story you told that bonny French creature I had my eye on at Falkland Palace last summer?" Alexander growled. "Something about my wife and two sickly bairns being due to arrive at the castle at any moment, if I recall."

"If you think we will show you any mercy…"

"…You can just put it out of your mind," the older brother finished. "You've been able to escape unscathed before. But 'tis time that you reap what you've sown, now that this Tess has caught your eye."

Alexander didn't even see the kick coming until he found himself hurtling toward the stable wall. The other brother, being bigger, put up a tougher fight, but Colin managed to slip his grasp and press James's face into the dirt as Alexander fought to regain the breath knocked out of him.

"Now listen to me, you buggering peacocks," Colin warned, knowing his advantage was momentary at best. "'Tis true I've taken a few opportunities to torment you two in the past, but if you search inside your thick skulls, you might remember that you were never serious about any of those lassies. At best, you were thinking of a night or two of…well, whatever you were thinking of."

"Ha! Looking out for us, were you?" James laughed mockingly. "Our guardian angel speaks! Let me up, Lucifer."

Alexander lowered his voice. "Are you telling us that there is a reason why we shouldn't ruin your chances with this Lindsay lass while she is here?"

"Aye!" Colin spat out passionately. "If all I wanted was a roll in the hay, I would have wooed her on the island and let it end there. I'm thinking…well, she trusts me, and I can't let some senseless teasing by you two make her doubt her judgment."

"The devil, you say," James challenged, looking at him incredulously. "If you think you can win us over with such drivel—"

"Aye, if she trusts you, the lassie's judgment is a wee b—"

"I mean it." Colin pushed himself impatiently to his feet. "You didn't see her on that island. I did. I saw her frustration and confusion over who she was and what her future might be. I'm telling you it took great courage…and trust…for her to leave the May and come back here with us. Tess cannot afford to be doubting herself now. She is too vulnerable, as 'tis. Until she's at peace with her past, I feel…well, responsible for her. And that means with everyone out there, including you two flap-jawed, boneheaded apes."

"I think the lass must have fed you some kind of potion when you were on the May," Alexander said half-seriously.

"It may just be a fever," James suggested. "But you didn't, by any chance, inhale any odd-smelling smoke out there?"

"She didn't bewitch me, damn it!" Colin growled at the two amused men.

"So you say, brother," Alexander commented. "But from the moment we fetched you two from the island, you've had stars in your eyes."

"Bloody hell!" Colin barked. "Well, of course I'm…well, she's a bonny lass! But that's not…Och, by the devil, this is all confusing as hell!"

"So we see," James chuckled.

"Listen, you two! The most important thing is for Tess to find her people and get settled."

"Very well." Alexander replied, growing serious. "What do you want from us?"

"And what will you give us for it?" James added with a grin.

"I want no bloody mischief. Just your best behavior. And perhaps wee bit of respect."

"Nay, you go too far now," Alexander deadpanned.

"I mean it. I need a chance to figure out the best way I can help her. I need to spend time with her, to encourage her as a friend should." He glowered fiercely at the two men. "That is, without your childish comments and antics."

The two older brothers again glanced at each other first before James answered.

"Well, lad, this may just be the best way yet of getting rid of you. So, aye, I'd say you can count on us."

Fiona had assured Tess that she would be more than presentable should Lady Evelyn arrive even without advance warning.

But Tess had no idea what the mistress of Benmore Castle had up her sleeve.

Soon after Fiona had left, a cadre of the household workers arrived with a tub and buckets of steaming water. Never, as far as she could remember, had Tess experienced such luxury. As she soaked in the jasmine-scented bath water, she'd felt the soreness of her hours in the saddle melt out of her tired muscles. And she'd no sooner stepped out of the tub when Lady Fiona's seamstress and helpers had arrived at the door with strict instructions for measuring and dressing her.

Tess's old dress had been whisked away. Dressed in a new silk shift, the like of which she'd never before seen or felt, Tess stood dutifully on a stool. For what felt like hours, though it was probably only minutes, the old seamstress and her assistants tried on and pinned several partially made dresses—garments that Tess suspected had originally been intended for Lady Fiona's own wardrobe.

As they bustled around her, cutting and stitching, Tess had made polite conversation with the women. She'd enjoyed getting lost in their Highland accents when they talked among themselves. But at some point during this ordeal, Tess's gaze had turned longingly toward the deep billows of the brightly decorated bed. The mattress looked as puffy as a cloud.

"Will ye look at this bonny lass now!"

"I say one look at her by our lads, and she'll not be strayin' far from Benmore."

Tess hadn't even realized that the women were talking about her until the seamstress moved a looking glass and rested it against the wall.

"Look at yerself, lassie. Ye are sure to put the very moon to shame."

Tess didn't recognize the young woman staring back at her through the silvered glass. Never in her life had she worn such a fine gown. The ivory-colored bodice, laced with threads of gold, clung to her slender frame and then flared to a long, full skirt below the curves of her hips. The tight sleeves hugged her arms while the plush velvet cuffs extended over her fingers. Tess eyed the low neckline and blushed at the revealing sight.

"No worries about that, mistress." The seamstress must have followed the direction of her gaze. The woman moved to a chest and came back with a length of Macpherson plaid. In a moment, she'd artfully arranged it around Tess's shoulder.

"This is absolutely beautiful." Tess whispered in awe, staring at her reflection again. "But, to whom does this dress belong?"

"This one was to be Lady Fiona's—though she was only having it made up to please the laird. The same with those." The woman motioned toward a few dresses that were lying on the bed. "She wanted ye to have 'em...until we can make something to yer own tastes, mistress."

"But these are so beautiful!" Tess said shyly. "This is too much! I have been so much trouble already...and..."

"Nay, lass. The mistress is truly enjoying this." The woman sent her a toothless smile. "With no daughters to fret over, and with three braw and handsome sons who should be looking for wives, I'd say yer presence here is more welcome than ye know."

Tess tried to hide her blush by stepping off the stool. Chatting happily, the women went about their business of hanging the other dresses and cleaning up after themselves.

Looking for wives. Tess pressed her icy hands to her fevered cheeks as the words echoed again and again in her head.

The memory of her time with Colin on the Isle of May was branded forever in her mind. Every moment they had spent together, everything they'd said, the image of his smile, the gleam that crept into his deep blue eyes and set her on fire were all branded there as well.

She ran her fingers over the plaid scarf.

But Colin had plans of his own. He'd said it himself, and Tess had heard it again from Alexander on their way to Benmore. Colin had always wanted to be a sailor. He dreamed of taking command of his own ship and living a free and exciting life at sea.

She moved to the table beside the bed and touched the Lindsay brooch. Lady Fiona's words about the marriage of Tess's parents rushed back to her. She couldn't help but fear that perhaps her own marriage someday might be an arranged one. Her mother had left the Highlands after the death of her father, and Tess wondered why. What dark secrets did Ravenie Castle hold? She carefully pinned the brooch on the Macpherson wrap and decided that there was no point in tormenting herself with such thoughts now.

The seamstress and her helpers gathered all of their things and bid her goodnight. Lady Fiona had told Tess earlier that she would be sending someone after her as soon as the seamstress was done.

The noise of revelry in the Great Hall was loud when the two women opened the door to depart. She would know almost no one down there. She had been so far removed from crowds for so long. It was almost terrifying to think of being in an assembly of so many people. On top of that, Tess was uncertain even about proper customs and manners at table.

She looked in the mirror again and wondered for an instant if Colin would have anything to do with her, now that he was back among his own people. It would be only natural if he decided to distance himself from her now, but she found herself hoping fervently that he would not.

Tess gathered up her long dark hair and pulled it over one shoulder. Colin knew her. He understood her. There was no pretense between them. She no longer had a home, but when she was with him, she felt a sense of comfort that she wondered might be something akin to belonging. If only he would feel a fraction of what she felt for him.

Nay. Tess knew it was too much to hope.

Blast this foolish nervousness, Colin thought, staring at her door. What had he to be nervous about?

Everything…that's what.

Drawing a deep breath, he knocked.

She must have been waiting on the other side, for the iron-banded oak door swung open immediately. His breath was caught in his chest again at the sight of her.

In the golden light of dozens of candles spread around the chamber, she looked absolutely stunning. "Are…are you ready?"

"I am. But would you come in first?"

He knew better than to go inside, and he reminded himself now. Colin *knew* how flimsy his restraint was becoming when he came anywhere near her. Still, he found himself taking a step inside her room. He couldn't help himself.

"You look so...so..." Before he could finish the sentence, Tess had him by the hand and was closing the door behind him. "...Wonderful. But I do not think...what I mean is..."

Tess released him and backed away.

He was feeling like an abbey schoolboy. She wasn't looking too steady herself, either, Colin thought, watching her put distance between them.

"I missed you," he finally got out.

A deep blush colored her face prettily.

"You do look stunning, Tess." He frowned. "The problem is, I do not know if I care to trust my brothers with escorting you downstairs. I have been trying to—"

"You look wonderful, too," she interrupted shyly, but Colin didn't miss the way her eyes traveled the length of him. She took a step toward him, and he tried desperately to fight the urge to reach for her.

"I told my parents that I would..." His words died in his throat as Tess unconsciously tossed her dark mane back over her shoulder. The tartan wrap shifted slightly, revealing the swells of her ivory skin over the top of the dress. He swallowed hard. "I don't know what my mother was thinking. This won't do at all."

"What won't do?"

"This dress." Colin walked across the room with every intention of simply adjusting the wrap. But at the next moment, she was in his arms, and he drew her against him. Time hung suspended between them as his gaze caressed her face before settling on her lips. "It just needs..."

His mouth descended and gently brushed against hers. She was so soft, so beautiful.

Looking into his eyes, Tess raised a hesitant hand and touched her own lips before touching his, feeling the texture. The simple gesture made his heart pound in his chest.

Colin couldn't stop himself from kissing her again. This time, though, all the passion he had in him poured into the contact of their lips.

"This seems so right," Tess whispered breathlessly when they broke off the kiss. "I've wanted you do this for so long."

As her words registered, Colin's hands immediately dropped to his sides. Silently cursing himself, he tried to take a step back, but Tess touched his arm, her eyes holding his.

"What is wrong?"

She was like an angel, but with the images running through his head, he felt like Auld Nick himself. He was the only one she knew here—the only one she could rely on. And here he was, ready to take full advantage of that trust. He finally managed to find his voice.

"Nothing," he said gruffly. "I…I told my parents that I would escort you to the Great Hall."

"Of course." She couldn't hide the note of sadness in her voice. "I am ready."

"I've hurt you."

She shook her head and tried to turn away, but he took her hand. "Tess—"

"This is all part of this game, isn't it? The game that you said once that women play. I should not say…say what I feel. Honesty is not allowed. 'Tis all part of the education that I…that I lack."

"Nay, Tess. This is about me and how I feel about you. This is about caring for someone so much that you want to do everything right. This is about responsibility and even about protecting your good name."

"This is all…all…" She shook her head, and tears rolled down her cheeks. "I might lack much in the ways of the world, Colin, but I know when someone does not want me."

"That is not true. And nothing would give me greater pleasure right now than to show to you how much I want you." He gently wiped the tears off her face. "But I will not take advantage of you, Tess. I cannot let our attraction for each other move beyond the bounds of reason. There is so much that you need to work through right now. Making peace with your past. Finding your family."

"You are so noble," she whispered brokenly. "And I so wicked."

"You are anything but that. In truth, I am the wicked one for tempting you the way I have. I am truly sorry." Colin pressed his lips gently to the back of her hand he was still holding. "'Twill never happen again, Tess. I promise you. You need to know that you are safe with me."

"I do know that," she replied somberly. Pulling her hand away, she moved toward the door.

CHAPTER 11

*A*s they entered the festive Great Hall, the sounds of music and revelry filled the air. Great fires lit the fireplaces, and food and drink were being carried in by castle workers wearing bright ribbons and followed by ever hopeful dogs. A number of men playing bagpipes marched around the hall, and children from the village danced happily behind them. On every side, laughter and merriment surrounded the latecomers, and no one appeared to even notice their entrance.

Tess glanced at the long tables, filled with men and women of every generation. She saw the Macpherson warriors and sailors they had traveled with sitting among them. At the dais, the laird and his lady were obviously enjoying the festivities. Tess couldn't help but wonder if Ravenie Castle at one time had been like Benmore. She glanced at the long tables again. And for a moment she saw in her mind's eye different faces, a different tartan, another clan. A company of rowdy Highlanders sitting around one end of a trestle table with large trenchers of food before them. Their boots heavily stained. Their tartans covered with the dust of their travels.

Tess roused herself from her reverie as she realized a hush had fallen over the Hall. The musicians ceased their playing, and all eyes were upon her. Colin held on to her hand as she nervously tried to take a step back. She glanced down at the dress that had been intended for Lady Fiona. She stared at the Macpherson tartan that covered her shoulders and the Lindsay brooch that held it in place, and she wondered if the quiet were caused by an outsider wearing their plaid. She had not stopped even to consider the appropriateness of wearing the tartan. Her mind raced to think of what else could cause such a reaction.

"What have I done?" she asked Colin uneasily.

"You have stunned them with your radiance," Colin whispered reassuringly. "Because of all the stories, I think they were expecting either a wee wild child...or some haughty Lowlander like your mother."

"But I am neither," she murmured.

"I know that. And they realize it now, too. In addition, you are wearing a Macpherson tartan to boot. A bonny sight to their tired eyes, I'm thinking."

"Perhaps I should not..." Tess felt her cheeks catch fire. She tried to pull away. "Maybe I..."

Instead of letting her go, Colin pushed her gently toward the dais. Looking ahead, Tess realized that the laird and lady and their two elder sons were all standing now and waiting.

The Macpherson chieftain came around the table to greet them. "Finally I have the honor of introducing our own faerie to a grateful clan."

Tess dropped a low curtsy before the laird. "The honor is mine, m'lord."

Alec Macpherson took her hand, and his blue eyes were approving when he raised Tess up. He turned her to the silent crowd gathered in the Great Hall.

"'Tis my honor...my privilege...to give you the angel to whom we are all indebted for saving young Colin's life. With great pleasure, I introduce to you, my good clan folk, Theresa Catherine Lindsay, the only daughter of my friend, the late Sir Stephen Lindsay."

As the laird paused, the room suddenly erupted with cheers. Tess was embarrassed by all the credit she was receiving with no cause. Before she could gather herself together, though, the laird opened his arms and she moved unthinkingly into his embrace. His powerful bear-like arms wrapped around her. In a moment, he released her from the hug but still held her by the shoulders.

"Your father would be very proud to see you tonight, Tess." He placed a kiss on her brow, and Tess fought the emotions welling up inside of her. There was so much she needed to know about her father, about what had happened to him, about the secrets of Ravenie Castle. When the laird let go of her, she turned and found herself enveloped in Lady Fiona's arms.

"You look exceptionally beautiful. And you act as nobly as a queen," she whispered in Tess's ear. "No more fretting, child. You are ready for your lady mother...whenever 'tis you meet again."

The recollection of their kiss wouldn't leave Tess's mind. Hours later, she could still feel the tingling sensations on her lips and the pounding of her heart. At the same time, she was angry at herself for this weakness. Colin had told her in so many words that kissing her had been a mistake, that it wouldn't happen again. So then why was it she couldn't put it behind her?

Perhaps it would be better if she were to go, she thought, trying to convince herself. Perhaps, with some distance between them, they could both get on with what they had to do.

Tess tossed and turned in the deep feather bed for what seemed like hours. No matter that she was tired, sleep seemed destined to elude her. She finally gave up the struggle and sat up. A full moon had spread its light across the chamber floor like a carpet of blue silk.

Rising, she followed the lunar glow to the window and sat on the window seat. The valley and the endless hills beyond the panes of glass looked so strange and beautiful in the moonlight. As she looked out at the scene, she touched her lips and wondered where Colin was at this moment.

Forcing her thoughts away from him, Tess looked down at the curtain wall that surrounded the castle, and she tried to remember what it was like at Ravenie Castle. She had a vague recollection of a wee lass spending many nights just like this, a blanket around her to keep out the cold as she looked out at the world from her own quiet perch. There were prayers then for battles to be won and for warriors to come home through those hills to the south. The child would even doze occasionally, waking up with a start when her small chin would drop to her chest.

And then there was that night when violence had battered at the walls of Ravenie Castle. That night of tragedy when her life had changed forever. Tess's past—all the lost memory of her childhood—remained bound to that one night. All the secrets of what took place there still remained trapped within the walls of that castle. And there was mystery about it all that she sensed others knew of but would not voice. She had felt it in Colin's hesitation. She had heard it in Lady Fiona's tone tonight. She had certainly sensed it in the Macpherson laird's protective embrace.

The tragedy of what occurred had forced her to forget so much. But for Tess to remember again and move on with her life, she knew she needed to go back. She had to go to the place she'd once called home. She needed to see it through the eyes of the person that she had now become. She had no choice but to go and face the nightmare that has been haunting her.

And she needed to do all of this before she saw her mother again.

Whatever was left of Ravenie, Tess knew that the secret to her life lay buried there.

"But you only arrived here yesterday."

Tess looked into the water running clear beneath the arches of the stone bridge. The neat little village on the bank of the Spey had been bustling with activity. Three healthy looking little boys were wading at the edge of the cold water with fishing lines in their hands.

"It cannot wait, Colin. I have already spoken with your parents about it. 'Tis all planned. It only makes sense to go now—the day after tomorrow. If I don't do it now, I might not have a chance again for a long, long time."

"But 'tis at least six hours on horseback each way," he protested. Reaching the end of the bridge, they started up the steep hill toward the castle. "Longer, even, if the rivers are running high."

"The ride presents no difficulty. 'Tis shorter than the ride here." Tess asserted. "Besides, your father said that many times messengers went back and forth between the two castles in a single day. The laird has even arranged for a group of Macpherson warriors to escort me. I shall have no problem in making the trip."

She saw the disappointment in his face. She had not asked him to go. After last night, she did not want to pressure him into spending time with her—or feeling responsible for her. But now she wondered if he was thinking she wanted to run away—to get away from him.

"You are not truly upset that I wish to see Ravenie again, are you?"

"'Tis a matter of timing, Tess."

"Is it?"

"Aye. You only arrived and there is so much here that I want to show you. I guess I was hoping we could get to know each other without the pressures of necessities...and..."

She looped her arm through his. "I am only going for one day, Colin. And you told me yourself that I need to make peace with the past. In talking to your father and your mother, I learned a great deal about my family. Things I never knew. Things such as how much my own father loved me, and how his service to the king kept him away so much. Lord Alec told me, too, of the arrangement that led to my father's marriage to my mother. He told me again how unhappy they both were."

He slowed his steps, and Tess's voice wavered a little as she continued. "I have heard a great deal, but now I need to go and see it for myself. I must do this, Colin. Just as I need to see my mother, I also need to go to Ravenie and reconcile those memories of my father, of my childhood. I...I need to face the nightmares, too. I have to remember what happened and try to understand why it happened...try to make myself recognize who I really am, and if there is anywhere that I truly belong."

He stopped abruptly and turned to her. "You belong to..."

The rest of the words did not come. Colin's chin dropped to his chest for an extended moment. Tess was overwhelmed by the emotions that his action—that his unspoken words—brought forth in her.

She was stunned momentarily to realize that she *loved* him.

"You never again have to worry about where you belong." He finally looked up at her. His hand reached for hers, and he entwined their fingers.

Tess nodded gratefully but the raw emotions continued to play havoc inside of her. What had he been about to say at first? That she belonged to him? Nay, she thought in confusion. If he felt that way, he wouldn't let her go so easily. She gently removed her hand from his.

"I need to do this, Colin. I need to go back and see what it was that I left behind. But I also need to know that you understand."

"I do, Tess. I do."

Night still held both castle and river valley in the folds of its dark cloak. With the exception of the kitchen workers who'd roused themselves early to serve a morning meal to the warriors leaving for Ravenie Castle, the rest of the household was still sleep.

Seeing that she was not in the Great Hall, Colin took a trencher of food with him and went out across the torch lit courtyard to the stables. He could see the workers were saddling horses and bringing them out to the pen.

The shadows of the yard were deep, but he spotted her easily as she paced back and forth before the stable door, wearing her leather cloak and looking like a night nymph waiting to steal his heart.

Tess, however, was deep in thought and whirled in surprise seeing him. "What are you doing here?"

"That is no way to greet a man who plans to accompany and protect you on a long journey." He handed the trencher of food to her, and she had no choice but to take it.

"But you are not coming. The laird said that he will have someone—a company of your kin—to accompany me. But I never thought he would ask you."

"He didn't."

"Then why...?"

"I'm responsible for you. You saved my life. I owe you."

"Colin, I cannot allow any sense of debt you feel to push you into coming with me," she protested. "And in the matter of who is in debt to whom, you are the one who saved my life by bringing me—"

"Tess, please, let it go." He cupped her chin and looked closely into her beautiful dark eyes. "Let me put it this way, I cannot let you leave Benmore without me. I want to come. I have to come."

They gazed into each other's eyes for a long moment, and then Tess simply nodded.

He was grateful that she didn't press him further about his motives for coming. How could he explain something that he couldn't understand himself? Colin walked to the stables to check on the horses that were being readied. He'd had a lengthy talk about Ravenie Castle and the Lindsays with his father last night. He wanted to be ready for what they were going to face—whatever it was. He wanted to be ready for the Lindsay clan's reaction to Tess's appearance.

All Lord Alec had been able to tell Colin about Ravenie itself was that the place had never been repaired after the fire. Evelyn, claiming that there was no proof yet that Tess, the only heir, was truly dead, had left a steward there to oversee the holding and collect the rents in her daughter's name. As far as Colin's father had known, there had been no fighting by the Lindsay clan, no appeals to the king. From a distance it appeared that the people's heart had died with their chieftain.

"We shall *never* get there moving at the pace you're setting this morning."

Colin turned to the shadow of his brother approaching from the house. "What do you mean *we*?"

"I mean *we* as in I'm riding along." James stretched and gave a great yawn. "I've been down that way a few times of late, and I know the lay of the land. Why, there's a fine tavern just south of there on the Inverness road with the prettiest lasses this side of..."

"We're going directly to Ravenie Castle and back."

"I know that, you fool." James grinned and clapped his brother on the shoulder. "Our parents decided last night that it might be advantageous for Tess to make her first appearance among her people with several of the Macpherson brothers standing at her shoulder. They wanted Alexander to go, as well. But you know how attached the old goat is to his sleep. I, for one, was not about to have my throat cut by the beast for waking him up at this hour."

Colin certainly saw logic in his parent's thinking. No one knew what to expect when they arrived at Ravenie. And it would certainly help to have the Lindsays see another Highland clan as powerful as the Macphersons backing Tess.

"And don't worry. You have no need to lecture or threaten me about keeping my distance from Tess." James led his own horse from its stall.

"Is that so?"

The older brother smiled. "Actually, I've taken a liking to having Tess around. I was telling Alexander last night that, since her arrival, you've managed to somehow grow up. You are not quite so annoying to have around."

"You mean I haven't bothered you two since coming home about chasing every skirt from Elgin to Edinburgh."

"Aye, and that's a definite improvement." James pointed a finger at Colin's chest. "Keep it up, lad, and we might actually let you live."

CHAPTER 12

The sun was almost directly overhead. Riding side by side at the head of the group of warriors, they crossed over a green ridge and started down into the valley that Tess was told marked the beginning of Lindsay lands. Her anxiousness sat like a rock in the pit of her stomach. She glanced at Colin riding comfortably beside her. He had such confidence. She turned in her saddle and saw James riding and talking amiably to one of the older Macpherson warriors, halfway down the line of men. Everyone seemed so self-assured—everyone but her.

She turned to Colin. "Do you think the Lindsays already know that I am alive?"

"The way I understand it, they never gave up hope."

The closer they came to Ravenie, the more nervous she was becoming. "But do you think that they've heard that I am in the Highlands?"

"Despite the ruggedness of the land, news travels fast here. I would guess that as soon as we anchored and came ashore, someone was heading this way with every last bit of information they could collect about you."

They rode in silence for a few minutes.

"I don't know any of them," she finally whispered worriedly. "I cannot recall any names or faces.

"That worries you?" he asked.

"Aye. It troubles me greatly."

Colin nudged his horse closer to her side. His boot brushed against her leg, and his warm hand reached over and took her freezing one. "You are returning to them, Tess. This is more than anyone has done for them in eleven years."

Tess wished she could consider this a consolation, but she didn't. As short a time as she had been at Benmore Castle, she had seen in Lord Alec and Lady Fiona what a leader should be to their people. She did not remember her father to be able to guess what kind of laird he had been—or how well he had been respected by his clan.

Her mother, however, had left and never gone back to Ravenie. How could anyone care for their people by staying away for so many years?

The track they were following crossed another path ahead, and the two reined their horses to a halt. Colin let go of her hand and turned to James as he approached.

"Turning to the right here will take us directly to Ravenie Castle," the older brother told Tess. "The path bends around that forest grove and climbs to higher ground behind it. The path we're on goes straight over that brae through the farms and to the old village and tower where the clan chief originally lived…before the king gave permission for Ravenie Castle to be built. So if you'd like to go to the Castle…"

"I wish to go straight."

"We shall go wherever you wish to go." Colin replied with a nod, motioning the group to that direction.

She had lived a nearly solitary life for so many years on the Isle of May. Now she realized that *place* had very little significance. It was *people* that mattered.

The trail they took wound up a rocky brae toward an azure sky. With each passing moment, Tess's anticipation grew. At the crest of the hill, she brought her horse to an abrupt stop as she stared at the squalor that lay before her in the valley.

There were old huts made of stone and timber and sod in various stages of disrepair beside a grove of tall trees. Even from here, she could tell from collapsed thatched roofs that many were deserted. Though some fields had been planted, more lay fallow. She urged her horse down the slope behind Colin's steed. The land looked to be good for grazing, though there were few sheep and even fewer of the red, shaggy cattle she seen so many of around Benmore Castle. A wide stream snaked through the countryside.

In a few moments, they'd drawn near the first of cottages nestled into the side of the brae.

"Where do you think these people have gone?" Tess asked, eyeing the burned hut. A flap of stiff, blackened leather hung by a single strand in the doorway of the abandoned cottage.

"Crofters won't stay where they are unprotected." Colin waited as she rode closer to the buildings. "These folks might have moved down into the village."

Protection. These people had no *protection*. Tess felt the knot tighten in her stomach. She followed Colin as he continued on down the path. James pushed ahead of the others to ride beside them.

"Beyond that glen just ahead, the village lies. Would you like me to send a couple of men before us?" he asked Tess. "I shall go myself to tell the village folk that you are coming."

She shook her head adamantly. "I don't want a prepared welcome."

"I shouldn't worry much about that." Colin said. "But without giving them any warning, there is no telling how they'll..."

"Please don't," she interrupted gently. "I appreciate your offer, though. But I cannot ask for their acceptance. I have to earn it."

Tess pushed past the two brothers and slowly continued toward the village. She had thought the greatest test of her courage would be facing her mother. But this was much harder.

She took one last look at the abandoned farm. Suddenly, there seemed to be so much more at stake.

A moment later, she heard the hooves of the Macpherson horses behind her. She turned in her saddle and found Colin and James riding right behind her. Tess took strength from Colin's reassuring nod.

At the crest of a hill beyond the glen, she reined her mare again to a halt. At the bottom of a long gentle slope, beside a broad creek, lay a partially ruined tower house. Stretching out from what had once been a stone curtain wall, a cluster of fifty or so cottages formed a village on both sides of the water. On this side of the brook, at some distance from the outer line of huts, an orchard of fruit trees ran in neat rows up the hillside, and a small herd of the shaggy, red cattle grazed in open pastureland. On the other side of the valley, she could see good-sized flocks of sheep and newborn lambs.

"That is Ravenie to your right."

At James's announcement, Tess looked past the village. There, Ravenie Castle loomed proudly on the high ground overlooking the countryside. From this distance, she could see no sign of the fire, no indication that there ever was any damage.

Tess looked back at the fields and at the briskly running stream and, finally, at the village. "You say the Lindsay chieftain once lived at the tower house?"

"Aye. They call it the Tower. The castle itself is only as old as your father would have been. I believe your grandfather built it."

The happy shrieks of children drew Tess's gaze back to the huts, and the edges of her mouth turned up in a smile as she watched a dozen, small, barefooted urchins running in playful pursuit of a dog. She wondered if in her own childhood, she had been allowed to come and play in the village.

Tess's attention turned to the groups of men and women who seemed to have stopped the planting they were doing. They were all staring up the hill in their direction.

"They won't be afraid of Macpherson men, will they?" she asked James, suddenly concerned.

"Macphersons have never raided these lands before. And in times of hardship, many Lindsay crofters have traveled west and taken shelter among our people. There is no reason for them to be fearful now."

But some of the Lindsays seemed definitely agitated, Tess thought. She watched as a number of them started quickly down toward the village.

She led her horse through the groves of fruit trees that lined the steep hillside. The rest of the group followed behind her. Breaking out of the trees into one of the upper pastures, Tess reined in her mount and called a greeting to half a dozen workers who were watching the riders approach.

None raised a hand in welcome. None called a greeting. And the Macphersons were not the object of these people's hard stares. Tess was.

She swallowed the painful knot of disappointment that was threatening to choke her and rode slowly past the silent throng.

"Perhaps we should go to the castle first," James suggested.

"She has to face this. 'Tis best that she do it now," Colin said in answer to his brother. But Tess could have spoke them, as well. She was glad that he understood.

As they approached the village, she could see more people coming down from the fields to the edge of the path. Regardless of whether they were man or women or a child, their expressions were the same...and they were far from friendly. An arrowshot from the edge of the stream, as dozens of onlookers watched, Tess climbed down from her horse.

Colin and James reined their steeds in beside her. She handed the reins to James. The rest of the Macphersons were lined up behind their leaders.

"I would like to walk from here alone."

Colin instantly opened his mouth to object, but then closed it without a word.

"I just ask for a little time," she said softly, reaching up and taking his hand. "This is all part of what I have to face...alone."

He nodded, but his fingers held on to hers for an extended moment before he finally let her go.

Tess turned to face her destiny.

Straight ahead, she could see that the narrow road that led to the ruined tower house was crowded with people. Tess took a deep breath and stepped toward the eerily silent assembly.

The same children that had been running happily before now moved to stand beside their elders. Tess looked down at the bare feet and dirty faces, at the rags that they wore as clothes. This close, she saw other things, as well. The look of hunger was pronounced in some faces. There was illness in others. There was also curiosity and caution and even despair.

She looked hard at the poor condition of the cottages…and she knew. What she saw here was so different from what she'd seen at Benmore Castle. These people had clearly been ignored and neglected by those who had promised to protect them. For too long the people themselves had been abandoned.

As Tess approached the first line of cottages, a scrawny dog of black and tan approached, hackles up and growling in obvious nervousness. Without retreating a step, Tess held out her hand, palm flat, welcoming the animal and his scrutiny. After a moment of sniffing, the dog wagged his tail and retired to his owner with the air of a victorious warrior.

With her head held high and her back straight, Tess walked farther down the road. With every step, she met people's gazes, and they made way for her. Almost to the tower house, she came upon a market cross. She stopped and turned around as the crowd closed in behind her. She turned completely around and looked into the circle of faces.

"I am Tess," she said gently and yet loudly enough for everyone to hear. "Most of you do not know me. Or if you do, you may only remember me as a child." She took a deep breath and tried to will away the doubts that were chilling her bones.

"I left here…" She shook her head. "I left *there*." She pointed to the castle on the ridge. "I left there eleven years ago…the same night that my father was killed."

Tess cleared her throat and struggled to organize her thoughts and her words. But everything had become a jumble of emotion within her.

"I don't know if 'twas the tragedy that I witnessed here or what happened during a terrible sea storm after, but when I washed ashore on the Isle of May, I had no memory of who I was or where I had come from." She looked into somber faces. "I was found by an old couple that were the keepers of St. Adrian's shrine. They were the folk I stayed with for all these years."

An old man leaning on a crutch nodded instantly at the mention of the shrine.

"While there, I thought 'twas my fate to remain forever on that island, taking care of a handful of sheep and a weary pilgrim or two every summer. I thought that was the life I was destined to live. And I would have done exactly that if it had not been that the youngest son of the Macpherson laird had one day washed ashore, as well." Tess glanced in the direction of Colin. He was sitting on his horse, eyeing the crowd warily. James and the other Macpherson men sat behind him

"'Twas he who identified the Lindsay brooch I had. 'Twas he who made me realize my nightmares of fire and horror were really a part of my past." Tess looked at Colin again, and her voice softened. "And 'twas he who told me that all of you were still here."

She looked at the faces again, held their gazes, sought their response. "I was made to realize that I was not alone, as I thought. That perhaps if I were to seek the people of the Lindsay clan, that if I were to explain to you that I was no different than you, that I too had been displaced and abandoned for the past eleven years…then perhaps you would take me back. Perhaps I would be given the opportunity of finally knowing my own people."

Silence once again threw its heavy wing over the crowd. Tess managed to hold back the tears despite the desperation that twisted her insides. The group continued to stare.

Then, a shuffling sound came from her left. She turned and saw an older man pushing through.

"My name's Robbie. I was the cook up at the castle when ye were a wee lass. I remember ye clutching at the skirts o' yer nursemaid, Elsie, and following her everywhere about the place." The man leaned his weight heavily on a stick that he was using for walking.

The memory was vague, like a scene she had perhaps imagined, but Tess voiced it. "I remember falling over a bucket of water and oats and nearly putting out the kitchen fire."

"Ye didn't fall, lassie. Ye jumped."

A rumble of laughter rolled across the crowd.

"Ye were always sure to be into a bit of mischief when ye were a wee thing." A middle-aged woman announced with a smile from the opposite side of the gathering. "I was one of the serving lasses that would come up daily from the village. I remember the day ye were trying to climb down the wall of the castle from yer room. Ye were caught on a ledge halfway down and didn't know to go up or down… and at the same time ye were refusing to cry for help."

Tess had never been afraid of climbing the cliffs on the May, and now she knew that her adventurous spirit had its origins here. "I wish I could remember your name."

"Lil." The woman smiled affably. "I fetched one of the grooms. 'Twas Rory. The two of us helped you down."

"I was the one she fetched." A man standing next to her said. "Ye were worried about some birds that were nesting on the ledge outside your window, lassie. D'ye remember?"

Tess took a step closer to the couple. She looked closely into the man's face. There was a flicker of recollection. "Horses. Somehow I see you where there are horses."

"Aye, mistress. 'Twas I that taught you to ride."

Someone else called out another story from the crowd. Another spoke out. Tess started to remember a sound, a name, a face. More than ever before, something sweetly familiar wrapped a blanket of warmth around her. The coldness that she had sensed before among these people dissipated like a morning mist.

She felt a tug at her skirt and looked down into the dirty face of a little girl beaming up at her. Tess opened her hand, and the child took it, nestling against her legs.

The first tear escaped. Then another.

Everyone seemed to be speaking at once, and Tess looked about her, realizing that no longer was she confronting a crowd. She had become a part of them.

An ancient woman hobbled toward her and clutched Tess's hand and brought it to her lips.

"I'm Bella. I was Elsie's mother. Your nursemaid was one of the castle folk who took you away the night of the attack. I know now that she was lost at sea with the rest of them."

With that, Tess broke down and cried as Bella wrapped her in a warm embrace.

At one point Tess looked across the throng of people and could no longer see Colin. Anxious, she searched the crowds again and found him this time speaking with some of the Lindsays. James was beside him too and some of the other Macphersons. All had dismounted and joined in the crowd. It was like some happy gathering of clans, and she relished the thought.

Tess felt the tug on her hand by the young child still standing with her. The girl pointed toward the castle.

A sudden change came over the demeanor of the villagers. Some folk quickly separated from the others and hurried back toward their huts. Others simply backed away until Tess caught sight of a rider and a half dozen armed men on foot who were approaching the market square on the road coming down from the castle. None wore the Highlander's kilt, dressed instead in Lowland breeches and chain shirts. Even from a distance, she could see that all were heavily armed.

"'Tis Flannan," the child murmured, half hiding behind Tess's skirt.

Tess turned to Bella, who was still standing near her. "Is he someone who knows me?"

The old woman shook her head. "He is the steward of Ravenie. Yer mother sent him from the Lowlands, lassie. He runs the castle and manages the land, and collects rents from the crofters in yer name. He has been here near ten years…maybe more."

The severe looks Tess had received on her arrival were nothing compared to the hostility that charged the air now.

"Is he a just steward?"

Bella's back was bent with age, but the woman still managed to raise her gray eyes to Tess's. "Maybe in the eyes of whoever he collects the rents for in the Lowlands. He doesn't give a rush about any of the folk here. He takes what he says we owe, and turns out those who cannot pay. We are here to serve him and his mistress, he says. We are to work and not complain. 'Tis the way of the world, he says. 'Tis the way of things here, to be sure, since the laird's death."

"Could you do nothing?"

"We chose leaders over the years to speak for the clan, but it made no difference."

Anger like none she'd ever experienced burned in Tess. In her name, in her mother's name, these people had been treated unjustly for ten years. She handed the little girl to Bella and approached the men.

The crowd continued to back away, forming a large circle as Flannan and his men reached the open area around the market cross. Tess didn't have to turn to know Colin had moved behind her. To her right and left, she saw Macpherson men keeping a watchful eye.

Flannan was approaching middle-age, bald with an enormous belly that sagged over the thick belt he wore over a greasy doublet and breeches. Tess noted the swagger of the armed men with him. Bullies, one and all, she thought angrily as they drew their swords and leaned on the hilts, the points buried in the dirt.

Tess was not deterred though, and she continued to approach. The steward's small eyes focused for a moment on Tess, but he made no move to get down from his horse or acknowledge her.

"Are you Flannan the steward?" She came to a stop a few steps away.

He looked over Tess's head, at whom she could only guess was Colin. "My men brought me news of some travelers passing through the village. Macphersons, they said." He gestured to the armed men to his right and left. "We are much better prepared to receive company at the castle. These lazy bastards need to be planting the fields."

"You haven't answered my question," Tess called, taking a step closer. If he knew about the Macphersons being here, he must have been told about her, too. Perhaps, she considered, he hadn't heard, though. Deciding to give him the benefit of the doubt, she introduced herself. "I am Teresa Catherine Lindsay. I believe 'tis in my name that you are steward of this holding..."

"What are you looking at, you filthy curs?" the steward shouted at the crowd. "Back to the fields."

A few people shuffled nervously, but no one retreated.

"Are you just going to ignore me?" she shot at him, growing livid at his insulting behavior.

The steward turned the head of his horse away and murmured some orders to the man nearest to him. Tess was too angry to think through any consequences. She started toward the man, only to stop in shock as everything exploded with activity around her.

Colin shot past her and had a grip on the back of the steward's belt in an instant. With one quick jerk, the fat steward was off the horse and on his hands and knees in the dirt.

There was a brief and short-lived scuffle between the Macphersons and Flannan's armed men, but the Lowlanders were no match for Colin, James, and the others...including the Lindsays who had joined them. In just a few moments of struggle, the Lowlanders had been overpowered.

Tess was not naïve enough, though, to think the battle was done. She was certain Flannan had more men at the castle.

"Would you care to answer your mistress's questions now?" Colin was standing behind the steward. The man had pushed himself off his hands, but still was on his knees. He cast a quick look at his subdued cohorts before scowling at Tess.

"I would have answered her to begin with if I thought the lass was telling the truth. She is no daughter of Lady Evelyn's." The steward pushed himself to his feet and spoke to the Lindsays that had once again surged forward to watch the spectacle before them. "This creature is nothing more than an imposter paid for by the Macphersons. See for yourselves! She was brought here to trick you fools." He turned and pointed an accusing finger at Colin. "Leave it to these pirates to think of a way to steal what is yours."

CHAPTER 13

"**S**he will hate me. She will think me the most horrible of mothers." Lady Evelyn continued to pace back and forth across her bedchamber. "And what happens if she decides that she does not wish to see me? What should I do if she remains in the Highlands with the Macphersons and the rest of those animals?"

"If she is truly who she says she is, then she will understand." David Burnett reached for the willowy woman's hand and forced her to stop. "If this young woman is *truly* Theresa Catherine, then she will come to you."

"'Tis she. I just know 'tis Theresa. For a long time, I have known that she would come back." The mother's fair features were flushed. She tugged her hand free and walked to the narrow window overlooking the courtyard. "Everything makes sense—where she was found to what age she claims to be. I've known this was coming for a long time."

Burnett's strong arm encircled Evelyn's waist, and he pulled her against his chest. His voice was soothing and reassuring in her ear. "We have done everything that we can, right now. You have answered her letter. I have sent a group of my most trusted men to Benmore Castle to escort her back. There is no reason to fret over this until she arrives at our gate."

Evelyn turned in the warrior's arm. Her hazel eyes glistened with tears. "Are you certain about this? About everything we are doing?"

"Aye, my dove," David assured her. "Just leave everything to me, and all will be well."

Nothing that Flannan said affected Tess in the slightest...except to make her want to correct the problems here even more. She turned to her clan.

"I find this man lacks the spirit and the good intentions my father had for our people while he was alive. I find this steward grievously at fault for his treatment of you over these past ten years. Now…who will help us restrain him and his men? Who will help us take back Ravenie Castle?"

A deafening cheer filled the market square as the entire village stepped forward. The steward, having realized his mistake, scrambled to take shelter behind the Macphersons, the same people he'd accused only moments ago.

In moments, Colin had divided the villagers into groups. Some were sent with James and handful of Macpherson warriors up to the castle. Others were assigned to see to Flannan and his henchmen in the village. There were many, though, who approached Tess on their own. Young and old, men and women—the noose around their spirits finally loosened—all were excited to talk to her and to make suggestions. All wished to know if she planned to stay.

Tess wanted to, but she had other things that demanded her attention before she could think about that.

Those remaining at Ravenie Castle who were loyal to the steward gave way to the combined force of Lindsays and Macphersons without a struggle. Most that James and the others encountered in the castle were from the village, anyway. To be sure, all of the Lindsays were fed up with the steward's treatment of their people.

All that Flannan's men asked for was permission to leave.

"I believe we should let all of them go," Tess told Colin with conviction. "Flannan included. My family is the most responsible for the hardship and the damage that has been done here. Though she has been absent all these years, my mother should have had someone checking on the steward. But she didn't."

She shook her head and watched the celebration that had been going on since midday.

"Don't torment yourself about the past," Colin said firmly. "None of that was your doing. You shall make these people forget their hardships. Anyone can tell that your arrival has already given new life to the Lindsay clan."

Tess looked up and their gazes locked. "You make me believe in myself."

"As you should." He gave her a smile that warmed her blood and sent tingles through her body. "Everyone here sees how special you are. 'Tis time you started believing it, too."

Tess beamed at him. "You are...you are a true friend."

A few days ago the words Tess had just spoken would have been enough for Colin. He would have been quite content to be considered her friend. But now, as he heard the words tumble from her lips, he knew it was not enough.

He had seen her courage in action today. While he fought back his own fears for her safety, she had walked into the midst of a mob that looked like a pack of hungry wolves. She hadn't known it, but his hand had never left the hilt of his sword until he'd seen the first sign of acceptance by the Lindsays.

"I believe I've found my home," Tess told him. "There is no doubt in my mind that this is where I belong."

He nodded, working hard to hide his own feelings at this important moment in her life. He gestured to where Flannan and some of his people were being held. "I'll make sure an escort of Lindsays and Macphersons convey these curs to the southern borders of your land. I do not believe you will hear from them again."

She looked around. "Having seen your village at Benmore Castle, I know there is a great deal to be done here."

Colin followed the direction of her gaze. "Aye, but this is good land. And James tells me that only a section of the castle was burned. The rest is solid and livable. You should probably take a ride up there and see it for yourself."

She turned toward the celebrating crowds. "I wonder what it would be like to live here, in the village. 'Twould be only right to find some use for this tower house."

"Nothing is impossible. Perhaps with a few good masons, and..."

"Will you stay with me here? Will you help me to start again?"

Colin abruptly stopped and looked at her. Tess's beautiful face was flushed. Her eyes were dark pools, so clear that he could see his own reflection in them.

For the first time in his life he had come to the realization that no other plans, no other dreams, no grand adventures in the world meant a thing to him if he couldn't have Tess. But at the same time, the uncertainty of his position as the third son, and *her* position as the sole heir to Ravenie Castle was suddenly gnawing at him.

"Tess, there is a great deal that...that..."

"I mean...temporarily," she said, dropping her hand in embarrassment. Her face was even redder than before. She hurriedly looked away when the first tears slipped down her cheeks. "I never intended to interfere with...with your plans. I just thought that if you have few days to spare, you might perhaps like to come back with me and…and…help me get started."

"Wait, Tess." He took her arm before she could walk away. "There is a great deal that you and I need to—"

Unfortunately, James took that exact moment to approach them. "The afternoon is advancing, you two. If we are to make it back to Benmore tonight…" He stopped, recognizing that he had walked in at a bad time. "Am I interrupting something?"

"Aye, you are."

"Nay, you are not."

Colin and Tess had spoken at the same time. James looked curiously from one to the other.

Tess shook her head at Colin before turning to James. "I should like to stay, but at the same time my mother is expecting me to be at Benmore. If, by chance, she herself would travel to the Highlands… well, I doubt she would ever come to Ravenie Castle. And yet, I am concerned about leaving. I think we are needed here."

Colin was far from ready to leave her here by herself. "Now that the Lindsays have formed a clan council, they will keep things here under control in your absence. However, we can also leave behind a few of our own men to help and assist them until you get back."

"Thank you," she said quietly. "I think we should plan on spending the night here, though. Would that be any problem?"

"Nay, Tess," James replied. "No problem at all."

Her eyes, taking on a worried look, scanned the villagers. She nodded absently and walked toward a group nearest to them. The old woman called Bella was at the center of the group, and Tess went directly to her.

Colin realized he must have been too absorbed in his attention to Tess, for James seemed to have repeated a question that he hadn't heard even the second time.

His older brother poked him in the ribs. "Why don't you admit it and be done with it?"

"Admit what?"

"That you are in love with her."

No denial rose to his lips.

James let out a low whistle. "Come now, brother. While you're at it, admit that you want to spend the rest of your life with her. Marriage, children, happily ever after. You know there is nothing that says the youngest son cannot marry first."

Colin turned abruptly and strode away. James followed.

"I never thought I'd see the day, but you are far, far gone…and don't deny it. You were probably sunk the moment she dragged you out of the water."

For some reason, James's words lacked the note of ridicule that Colin would have expected.

"So what are you doing tormenting yourself and her? 'Tis obvious that she wants you...perhaps loves you back, for all I know of such things."

"The whole damn thing is too complicated," Colin snapped, his tone harsher than he'd intended. "I don't have time to worry about such foolishness now."

James's large hand landed on Colin's shoulder. The older brother's gray eyes were deadly serious when Colin looked at him.

"You don't want to be spending the rest of your life regretting this moment." James lowered his voice. "Don't forget the family that she springs from. Lowlanders and Highlanders. A marriage by contract. Two unhappy, distant people thrown together for the purpose of property. Why, not that I'm an expert, mind you...but I think there's not a shred of romantic feeling in that whole arrangement. And I'll tell you something else..."

Colin waited, frowning fiercely.

"Once her mother takes charge of the lass, not you nor Tess herself will be deciding her future...*that's* for sure."

Colin felt ill at the truth in James's words. Physically ill at the thought of losing her.

"If you don't have time to work your way through this 'foolishness' as you call it, then just think of what lies ahead for her. Colin, lad, I'm not speaking lightly now. If this is what you truly want for your future, don't waste a moment."

As the Lindsay clan folk celebrated their liberation, Tess agonized over the thought that she'd practically begged Colin to stay with her at Ravenie. Mortified, Tess made certain that she didn't have another moment alone with Colin for the rest of day. Later, she gladly accepted Bella's offer of spending the night in her cottage.

Emotions were running high the next morning as they prepared to leave the village. A half dozen of the Macpherson men were to stay. It was clear to Tess, though, that the villagers were feeling far different without the heavy lash of the steward hanging over them.

She'd promised to come back after her meeting with her mother. She believed she would. And she was relieved to know that her people believed her, too.

"I know you have set your mind against it," Colin moved his horse next to hers as everyone mounted up. "But you should at least consider riding up there and looking in at Ravenie Castle before we leave."

He was all seriousness this morning. Tess wished she could have such tight control over her own emotions.

"And I am not suggesting it because I want to persuade you to live up there instead of down here." He was speaking only to her. "The fire in that castle and the murder of your father are a part of your past. There are decisions you will need to make when you come back. I think you'll have a much easier time doing that if you have settled *everything* that hangs over you from the past."

Her first impulse was to reject his reasoning and simply ride away, but common sense prevailed. Tess *was* curious about that night—about the fire and the attack.

Tess gave a nod of resignation. "Will you ride with me?"

Colin's tender look of agreement—the way he reached over and gently squeezed her hand—only managed to confuse her more. She loved him so much that it hurt to be around him, knowing the end of their days together was in plain sight. Everything about their situation was baffling. One moment, he was so aloof and distant, and the next he could be so warm and compassionate.

"Can we see Ravenie Castle and then come back and leave by the way of the village?" she asked finally. "When we leave here, I want the last image I carry with me to be these people and this place that I want to come back to. Not the place I have been having nightmares about for so many years."

He nodded. The devil take him, he thought, if he didn't win a prize for understanding. If he didn't get a chance soon to talk to her, though—to tell her how he felt—he'd surely explode. By 'sblood, he'd felt like a tongue-tied fool yesterday when she'd asked him to stay! And then, once he'd gathered his wits about him, Tess had avoided him. It was obvious she had made herself unavailable for the rest of last evening. And the night had been hell. He had tossed and turned until almost dawn.

Colin looked around at the other men gathered nearby. Now was not the time, either. Bloody hell. Shaking off his brooding thoughts, he tried to focus on what they had ahead of them this morning. Perhaps once she'd seen the castle, they'd have a chance to talk.

After asking James to keep the men in the village, the two of them rode up toward the castle.

Ravenie Castle was built on a rocky ledge surrounded by a dry moat that surrounded the stout curtain walls. To get to the bridge that led to the low arched entrance, they rode up a long and winding road.

"Some of the history of this place will never be truly known, I fear."

She spoke quietly, taking in the wild terrain of the surrounding hills.

"You are talking about the attack on the castle. About the night of your father's murder."

She nodded. "I asked Bella. There never have been any credible answers to it. The Lindsays were not feuding with any of our neighboring clans. As far as the villagers knew, Sir Stephen was well liked and respected in the Highlands. Even more strange, the attack came only on the castle and not on the village. In fact, the people down there didn't know anything about it until someone saw the flames mounting up to the sky."

"One would think that the castle would have been better protected. I went up there last night." Colin said. "There is this ditch to cross, then a banded oak gate and a portcullis, and armed gatekeepers. How could a group of men get inside the walls unnoticed?"

"They didn't just get inside the castle walls. They were inside the laird's chambers." She shivered uncontrollably. "My father was stabbed in the back. That tells me that they...they were waiting for him. Maybe they were even there *before* he arrived that night."

"I have been asking some questions of my own since yesterday, too." Colin added. "Amid all the chaos of the fire and the shouts of the laird's murder, there was very little fighting. This wasn't a case of the castle coming under the siege and taken by force. Nothing was taken. All that anyone remembers seeing afterward was a half dozen men dressed in an array of Highland gear fleeing into the night."

"Unidentifiable Highland gear," she repeated. "Bella said no clan could be accused afterward. 'Twas as if a band of outlaws just appeared in the castle, murdered my father for no apparent reason, and then disappeared."

Their horses had slowed. Tess saw the drawn portcullis and open gate of Ravenie Castle, and her heart started drumming in her chest.

There were dark, pungent pools of stagnant water in the ditch around the castle. She remembered the smell from her childhood. As she started slowly toward the bridge, her gaze traveled up the two stone towers facing the valley. The west tower was visibly burned. That was where her father had been killed. Her gaze never wavered from the blackened stones—from the slits of windows where she could see the sky peering through from the other side.

The wind blew in from the west and brought with it the earthy smell of stables and horses. Smoke from a wood fire in one of the chimneys reached Tess, and suddenly she found herself drifting back in time.

She could smell the smoke—taste it, even. Tess looked at the window where the laird's chamber had been and could see flames racing out.

There were cries for help. Chaos surrounded her with darkness and flashes of torchlight. Terrified, she wanted to run.

Her horse pawed the ground, snapping Tess out of the nightmarish state.

"I don't think you shall want to desert this place completely," Colin offered, waving to servants who were coming out of the doorway that Tess now remembered led to the Great Hall. She touched her brow and found it covered with sweat. "Where 'tis, sitting here on the hill, the castle offers a clear view in every direction. You need this for your own security and for the people who live in the village below."

She somehow managed to respond to the people's greeting, but remained on her horse, telling them that they needed to be riding to Benmore Castle and wouldn't be going into the keep. As the workers moved off, Tess could feel her heart continuing to pound. She turned to Colin.

"Do I need to do anything to the castle if 'tis just to be a place to keep watch?"

"Nay, you don't need to do anything, but—"

"Very well. I have seen enough. Let's go."

He reached over and took the bridle of her horse before she could turn away. "Your face is flushed. You are upset. Talk to me, Tess."

"I have nothing to say. Not here. I just want to leave." She could hear the note of terror in her voice. The courtyard was too small. There wasn't enough air. She tried to wrench his hand off the bridle, but he wouldn't let go. "I don't want to be here, Colin. I didn't want to come. I want to go now."

"Come, Tess. Let's get down from our horses. Show me around this place."

Temper arose in her. "I *want* to leave."

"Aye. And you will...in time." Completely disregarding her anger, he dismounted and lifted her from her saddle, as well.

As soon as Tess's feet hit the ground, she started walking straight for the gate. She heard his steps behind her, and she broke into a run. He caught her just as she entered the stone archway of the gate. She looked wildly toward the opening at the other end. She could see the iron points of the portcullis hanging ominously from the top.

"Let me go. I want to leave."

Colin's grip on her tightened. Tess felt trapped, and she immediately became a wildcat in his arms. Punching him, kicking him, she tried to break free, but he held her even tighter.

She did not scream, as she didn't want anyone to hear them. She didn't want her people to know that she was afraid of this place.

111

"I'll kill you when I get out of here," she hissed under her breath when he turned her in his arms, so she could face him. "I will take you onto a ship and push you overboard myself. And this time, I'll let you drown."

"Is that a promise?" The villain had the nerve to taunt her.

Instead of answering him, Tess kicked him hard on the shin. He winced but still did not let her go. Rather, he pulled her deeper into the darkness of the entryway and pushed her back against the hard stone. His body followed, pressing against her. She tried to struggle again, but then stopped as the tears began.

It was like an explosion of emotion in her, and one she could not control. One moment she was fighting him, hating him for bringing her here, and the next she was a sobbing mess, holding on to him and burying her face against his chest.

He let her cry. He held Tess in his arms and let her pour out the raw feelings. After some time, she realized that her misery had found a new fuel.

She was taking comfort in another human being. She was feeling the warmth of Colin's touch on her back, and she was nearly overwhelmed by the power of her own need. Holding him tightly, Tess stared at the glimpse of skin beneath the open collar of his shirt, at the solid pillar of his throat. Her hands inched their way across his broad and muscular chest, feeling his strength and his warmth.

And then she cried even more, knowing she couldn't have him.

It was some time before she became aware of the ridiculousness of her thoughts and pulled back. "I…I am…so sorry. I don't know what…what came over me."

Colin tenderly lifted her chin until she was looking into the deep blue of his eyes. "This is all part of settling the past behind you, Tess. Seeing, remembering, and then letting go."

"Remembering and letting go are the hard parts," she said brokenly.

His thumb gently brushed away the wetness beneath her eyes. "You need good memories of this place to replace those others."

"Nothing can wash away the nightmares from that night. Nothing!"

Colin looked more closely into her face. "Would you allow me to prove you wrong?"

"Allow you?" She gave a small laugh. "I would give anything to have something good to—"

The next breath was caught in her chest as his lips crushed hers. Then she forgot to breathe. For a mindless moment all she was conscious of was the consuming fire that was racing through her. This kiss was so unexpected, and yet so stunningly wonderful. She was afraid to move—

afraid to think—for the fear of breaking this magical moment.

Colin's mouth grazed the skin beneath her ear as her arms wrapped tightly around him. He kissed the hollow of her neck. He could feel her pulse fluttering wildly beneath his lips. There was so much that he wanted to tell her, about how he felt and what she meant to him, about how he could think of nothing else but her. But to his continued chagrin, Colin knew this was not the time. She already had too much that she had to deal with here at Ravenie.

His mouth returned to her lips, and he kissed her again before pulling back. "Come with me, Tess."

This time she walked with him into the bright, sunlit courtyard. She already knew that she would walk with him to the end of the world if he asked.

"Will you tell me what you have been hearing about this place?" Tess asked.

Instead of taking her to the burned section of the castle, he started toward the east tower.

"Forget about the place. Let's begin with its mistress. From all I heard down in the village, you were a wee faerie sprite when you were young." He gave her a devastating smile, and one arm wrapped around her waist, pulling Tess snugly against his side.

His smile was contagious, and Tess found herself relaxing a little. They walked up steps hewn out of solid rock.

"Now, what do you recall of where things are here?"

Finally being here, it was amazing how much of her memory was coming back. She told him what she could recall of the castle. They walked through the kitchens, looked at the old bread oven. She showed him the large stone trough for making bread dough. Here, the damage from the fire had obviously been repaired by the steward since, other than some blackened stones around the doorway, there was nothing else indicative of the tragedy.

"I have a vague recollection of this place with dozens of people bustling about and boys and dogs running in every direction." Tess moved away from him and ran her fingers along the edges of tables and hearths. "I can almost smell the bread in the morning. Robbie the cook, now I can almost see him, waving his stick about like a chieftain directing his warriors in battle. I also think that I wasn't supposed to come here. I think I was forbidden by my mother to roam around the castle by myself."

But Tess kept coming back. She was sure of that.

"Maybe I can convince Robbie to tell me some more stories of the mischief you got into when you were a wee bairn."

"I can save you the trouble." She moved into his open embrace. "I was a perfect child."

Colin kissed her again. But this time it was only a brush of lips—a teasing growl in her ear—before leading her into the next section of the keep.

The Great Hall spread across the area between the two towers. Two of the people who had greeted them outside came over now, obviously delighted to see that Tess had stayed.

"I couldn't let your mistress leave without showing me around this place first."

Tess was grateful for his explanation and for the way he engaged the old pair by asking a series of questions about the keep itself.

The Great Hall was older than she remembered, and the years that she'd been away had not helped it at all. A heavy blanket of dirt covered everything. There were birds nesting in the rafters and surly dogs eyeing her from dark corners. She glanced at the long trestle tables. Some of them were overturned and broken up. She spied the remainder of one in the huge fireplace by the dais.

Suddenly, the noise of the warriors coming back from days on the road filled her head—the clatter of dishes—laughter—the music of pipers. The warm amber light of torches and a log fire. A piece of her childhood, Tess thought, a fragment of long forgotten years. She wandered toward the dais.

The woven rushes on the floor were torn and filthy and reeking with disuse. Huge sections were missing completely. She looked for the colorful tapestries that once adorned the walls. Most were gone, though the badly tattered remains of one still hung between two windows. The Lindsay shield above the hearth was missing, too.

A strong draft swept through the room. Tess rubbed her arms to ward off the sudden chill…and then her gaze was drawn to the hearth. In her mind's eye, she could see herself—a young child again—frightened and uncertain. Her nursemaid had forced her to come downstairs and greet her father, who had been away for months. She drifted into the past.

The large man was pacing impatiently before the hearth. Though he wore no armor, she could see the stains of chain mail and leather clearly inscribed on the padded black tunic. A knot of fear tightened in her belly.

Sir Stephen Lindsay ceased his pacing as soon as he saw her.

"Tess!" he called out.

The young girl kept her gaze riveted on the man's heavily stained boots and wondered if the dark patches might have been someone's blood.

"Come closer, child."

Her feet would not move. Tess saw the laird's giant fist open and extend toward her in welcome. She shivered involuntarily at the memory of the stories she'd heard from her mother—stories of the furious killing of hundreds of men by these same hands.

"By the saint, my own Tess. Lord, you've grown so much since I last laid eyes on you."

He came across the rush-strewn floor, and Tess's eyes stung with tears. She had refused to see him the last time he'd come to Ravenie Castle, and there had been a price to pay for that. A young dog she had come to care for as her own had simply disappeared when the laird had gone back to the wars. Her father's punishment for loving an animal better than her own kin. Her mother had told her so.

"I've good news for you, Tess."

She stared at the boots moving closer, and the tears uncontrollably rolled down her cheeks.

"This time, I'm home to stay for a while."

The moment he laid a hand on her shoulder, every inch of the young girl's body went rigid. She bit her lip to keep from running.

"What's wrong, lass?"

He crouched before her, and she glanced up into his face. She wasn't prepared for the hurt she saw in those dark eyes that Elsie said were the exact match of her own.

"Why are you crying?"

Tess winced when she saw his large hand coming at her face. But the gentle brush of a callused thumb across her cheek was another surprise.

"I know you have not seen much of me, child. I've been doing the king's bidding for so long that you have every reason to think me a stranger. I even have a wee suspicion that you are afraid of me. But I plan to make up for the time we've missed, Tess. I am..."

He continued to talk, but the young girl's attention was fixed on her father's face. He didn't seem too frightening this close. She could smell leather and horses and salt air, and found herself oddly comforted by the scents. And then there was his voice, the way he was talking to her now. The gentle hush of it stirred in her mind a memory of a time when she'd been younger and he had been around more. She couldn't remember ever being terrified of him back then.

From the door of the Great Hall, her mother's exclamation was sharp
"Theresa Catherine!"

"Tess?"

She jerked around and looked in confusion at Colin for a moment. The castle workers were gone.

115

"What's wrong, Tess?"

"We were here. My father...my mother. She was angry because I had come down to see him." She looked back at the hearth. "I remember. He gave me a gift before I was sent back to my room. He gave me the jeweled cross for my sixth birthday that was the next day. He told me he would see me in the morning."

Tess didn't realize she was crying until Colin's arms wrapped around her. "They were all here." She looked up at him urgently. "I'm starting to remember."

She glanced nervously at the doorway that led to the west tower. "Will you come with me there?"

Colin's hand enveloped hers tightly.

Her steps were sure when the two walked to the ground floor of the tower. As they passed through the doorway and moved into the tower itself, she found herself in a great open space. Looking up, Tess saw that the upper floors were completely gone. But she could still see the weathered stubs of floor timbers protruding from the walls and the large fireplaces against the blackened stone walls.

"Our bedchambers were up there," Tess heard herself explaining. Even as she spoke, the past began to unfold, and she began to shiver. Pushing back the fears, though, she held tight to Colin's hand and continued. "It all started in the middle of the night. I woke up scared, thinking I'd heard a noise. But I wasn't sure. There was a faint smell of smoke in the air."

Colin's strong arm wrapped around her shoulders. He drew her against his side. "What did you do?"

"I picked up a candle and went into the corridor up there." She pointed. "There was the sound of a struggle coming from the laird's chambers next to my room. I saw the door open slowly on its heavy hinges. A moment later, I saw my father step out. He looked pale, his eyes black. He looked at me for an instant, his gaze distant. He stretched his hand toward me, and when I reached out...he pressed his brooch into my palm."

Tess swallowed hard. All the fragments of the nightmares came together now, and she drew a shaky breath.

"Then his sword dropped from his other hand, and he tumbled forward at my feet. The hilt of a dirk was sticking out of his back." Involuntarily, she tried to step back. Colin's arms embraced her. "I screamed and crouched down at my father's head. Before I could touch him, the other man appeared in the doorway."

"You saw him?"

She nodded slowly. "I saw the man who killed my father."

116

"Did you know him?"

"He wasn't anyone I knew."

Colin looked into her eyes. "Would you recognize him now?"

Tess hesitated for a moment, but then nodded again. "His face was streaked with blood. She let go of Colin's hand and opened her fingers wide before them. "These two...these two fingers were cut off. I think my father had done it, cut him...as there was blood dripping from his hand."

"Did he see *you*? Did he realize that you had seen his face?" Colin's tone had suddenly become urgent.

She nodded again. "Aye. He came after me—to kill me—so I know he did. My nightmares have all been about running away from this man."

"Your life could very well be in danger because of that." Tess heard the quiet warning, and then she saw Colin's hand go unconsciously to his dagger. "He could very well have been a Lindsay."

"I don't think he was, or I would have recognized him."

"There was no way you, as a child, would have seen or recognized every Lindsay clan member. The man—the people responsible for that night—could very well still be around here."

She shook her head. "I don't think so. I remember that as I was being taken away that night, I was told that my mother was in the same chamber as my father. That means that she must have seen the killer, as well. But she survived and nothing more happened to her."

"That is, assuming she *was* with the laird. 'Tis well known that your parents didn't have the best of marriages. She very well could have been in her own chamber...or somewhere else."

Tess couldn't argue her mother's whereabouts any better than she could argue about the kind of marriage her parents had.

"We have to get you out of here, Tess." Colin took her by the hand and pulled her toward the door. "My worry right now lies not with what your mother saw, but with keeping you safe. And standing alone within the crumbling walls of this wing is anything but safe."

CHAPTER 14

"Lady Evelyn is her mother," the laird said, "and she is not unreasonable in ordering Tess to the Borders."

"As her *mother*, one would have expected that she would not waste time in seeing her." Colin said heatedly.

"If you are saying she might have come to the Highlands, then I say we don't know her situation."

"I don't give a damn about her situation. Considering the significance of the news, what mother would not have started out instantly to see her *only* daughter."

"Lady Evelyn's letter says that she is jubilant at having regained her daughter."

"Some scribbling on a bit of parchment does not sound like jubilance to me. And to whom was the letter addressed, anyway? To you and not her own daughter. How can we stand by and allow Tess to be..."

Colin went on with his ranting, and Alec Macpherson leaned back heavily against the carving above the open hearth. When his son turned away momentarily, the laird eyed his wife's attempt at keeping a serene expression on her face in spite of their son's obvious unhappiness. Sitting across the room, Fiona was trying to look busy studying a drawing of a new storage barn she wished to have built. But Alec knew his wife had not given the drawing a moment's thought since they'd begun to speak to Colin...and she certainly wasn't thinking about it now.

The armed band of men that had arrived late last night were Burnetts, supposedly a distant kin to Tess's mother. With them, they had brought the cursed letter from Evelyn Lindsay, requesting...nay, demanding that Tess be sent immediately to the Borders in the company of these same men.

In a way, the laird had been happy that his sons had not brought Tess back from Ravenie Castle last night. He had not been looking forward to passing on the message. With good reason, he thought now, watching his youngest son.

When they'd arrived, Alec had requested that Tess come in to speak to them first. The lass had been quiet the whole time that he had explained her mother's wishes. As one would have expected from a dutiful daughter, the young woman had only given a curt nod to his statement that the Burnetts had orders to leave as soon as possible. After that, she had practically run from the chamber.

An instant later, Colin had stormed in, angry as a wounded bear.

"How does Tess feel about all this?" Fiona's quiet question drew the laird's gaze and momentarily silenced their son.

"You and father talked to her. How do *you* think she feels?"

Alec Macpherson started to answer, but caught the look Fiona was giving him and stopped. He'd seen this look before. They needed a united position—and it would probably be a more compassionate one than he was preparing to voice.

He shrugged. "The lass said nothing, Colin. She didn't say a word." He looked at his wife. "And I have been trained to read the unspoken language of only one woman. And that is your mother."

Fiona faced their son. "Are you telling us that you have come here with all these complaints without any regard for that child's feelings?"

"She is no child, mother. Tess is seventeen."

"Very well," she conceded. "You've come in here without knowing for certain the feelings of that young woman. Colin, you have no right to assume or to accuse or to complain when Tess might be perfectly happy with the arrangements made for her by her mother."

"But she is *not* happy," he asserted passionately. "She was crying when she left this room. She was very upset."

"Then perhaps you should go to her," the laird suggested. "I've always found that 'tis wise to go to..."

"Before you go anywhere near her," Fiona cut in, "Perhaps you should first sort out in your own mind the confusion that exists between you. 'Tis always better to offer comfort when one has a solution to a person's problems."

The laird almost asked 'What confusion?' but held his tongue as the lad seemed to understand perfectly what his mother was saying.

"I believe that has already been straightened out."

"Has it? And for how long?" Fiona pressed. "Is this the heat of the moment speaking? A momentary lapse into some sort of noble behavior?"

119

"I am speaking up because I love her."

The laird's head snapped in Colin's direction. "You...?"

"Love?" Fiona persisted. "Is this the love where two people spend the rest of their lives together?"

"If she'll have me."

"And what of your other plans? Plans of strapping on the sword of your ancestors. Years of sailing free? Of terrorizing every Spanish merchantman and treasure ship? Of..."

"Father didn't choose that path. He married and fell in love and settled happily. What is wrong with that?"

"Fell in love and married." Alec managed to get out the words before the two went at it again. "We shouldn't forget the order here."

His wife and son looked at him as if he'd just entered the chamber. Something told him this was probably not the best time to mention his tendency to become seasick.

"Go on. Go on," Alec encouraged his wife.

She turned back to her son. "It matters naught what your father did or didn't do. What about *your* dreams? *Your* plans?"

"We change, we grow, and we dream new dreams." Colin responded passionately. "Whoever I was before and wherever I wanted to go was shaped by what I had seen and where I had been. No dream I ever had looked beyond the here and now. Permanence played no part in my dreams. I know now that is because I had never found anyone who affected me as Tess has. I have no regrets for letting those dreams slip away. They could never make me happy now."

He started pacing again impatiently before them. "I know 'tis difficult for you to understand, considering that I am your youngest son. I know that the immature antics of my youth could cause you to think I am not serious. But I love her. The future means nothing to me if..."

"Stop right there. You should save this," the laird said solemnly, moving across the room and standing beside his wife's chair.

Colin's expression showed his puzzlement as Alec reached for Fiona's hand and the two exchanged a knowing look. The Macpherson chieftain recalled he had once been here himself, in this same room, twenty-seven years ago, presenting the same argument to his own parents.

"Colin, it makes us quite proud to hear how much you have come to care for this young woman." Fiona's gray eyes sparkled as she smiled at her husband before turning back to their son. "And your arguments are very convincing."

"When the right time comes, I believe you should use these same words to win her over," the laird added.

"I'm ready—"

"But considering her situation, if you were to propose now, Tess might think you are acting out of a sense of duty or honor." Fiona shook her head. "And I do not believe that is any basis for a lasting relationship."

"Not to mention that 'twould be impossible to explain any of this to Tess's mother so soon."

"Not that you are lacking in merit in any way." Fiona's tone sharpened with maternal defensiveness. "True, Tess has inherited a great deal of land, but you are a Macpherson and a Drummond, and royal Stewart blood flows in your veins. You will not lack for a fortune of your own, either, and you and Tess will together lift the Lindsay clan out of the difficulties they have long endured."

"We're not saying that your brothers wouldn't be glad to be rid of you." The laird smiled at his son encouragingly. "Nonetheless, you should wait a bit...at least until Tess is reunited with her mother. The lass needs to settle her past before she plans for the future."

"Come now, child. This is not the end of the world! You are going to visit your mother, and then you shall return to us."

Tess wished she possessed Lady Fiona's certainty. Wiping at her tears, she looked with embarrassment at the trunk full of clothing that had been prepared for her departure. Her gaze wandered to the velvet dress laid out on the bed, ready for her to wear during her last dinner at Benmore Castle. These good people planned everything for her—did everything for her.

When Tess had refused all help from the maidservants in getting ready for dinner, Lady Fiona herself had come up to see if she was well. And this was where she had found Tess, curled up in the window seat, lost in her misery and unable to stop the unending tears.

"Why don't you talk to me?" The older woman sat down next to Tess in the window. She wrapped an affectionate arm around her shoulder. "Don't you want to see your mother?"

"I do. I do!" Tess cried. "Please forgive me. I am behaving like an ungrateful wretch. I need to stop all this."

"Tell me, child, are you afraid that once you go down into the Lowlands, you shan't be allowed to come back?"

Tess nodded once before shaking her head. "I...I don't know. I'm certain that Lady Evelyn will want me to stay. But I have made up my mind. I have been independent for too many years for her to tell me...or force me to do anything against my will. The Lindsays need me, m'lady. And I need them."

"But you are so upset." Fiona pushed the loose tendrils of hair back off Tess's face. A thoughtful expression settled on the older woman's beautiful face. "Have you had a chance to talk to Colin since speaking to my husband and me today?"

Tess shook her head. After their moments together at Ravenie Castle, she had found herself daring to hope that perhaps he shared some of her feelings. That perhaps they might somehow have a future together. Still, though she knew in her heart the main reason for her misery was leaving Colin, she also hoped desperately that the truth of her feelings would not come out now.

Riding back from Ravenie, he had been constantly attentive of their surroundings. She knew it was her safety that he was concerned about, but as a result they had not had much chance to talk. And since hearing the news about her mother's message, she'd not seen him at all…with the exception of passing by him as she'd left Lord Alec and Lady Fiona. A horrible thought pierced her heart like an icy spike. Perhaps he wanted her to go. Perhaps, as far as he was concerned, Tess should pursue her own life and leave him to pursue his dreams.

"I heard that he had some errands that he was seeing to this afternoon," Colin's mother offered.

Tess was grateful for Fiona's explanation. "I have already taken so much of his time. 'Twas very kind of him…and James, too…to come with me to Ravenie Castle. I don't know what I would have done without their help."

"James told me how magnificent you were in facing your clan. He said you were quite impressive in both your courage and your eloquence in asking for their acceptance."

Tess shook her head shyly. She was hardly prepared to accept any praise in light of how weak she'd proven to be since returning.

"James is far, far too generous. But with the help of your sons, things have already changed on my father's land. And I realize now that the reason for this silly display of hysterics this afternoon—" She tried to smile. "—the reason is that you are the first true family that I have come upon for a long time." She shook her head. "The first true family that I have *ever* come across."

"I love you, child." Fiona Macpherson gave her an affectionate squeeze. She placed a kiss on her forehead, and Tess found herself trying desperately to contain her own surging emotions. "Tess, you are the daughter I have been waiting for. Now, come. Come and let's not allow this fine night to go to waste. There are people waiting for us downstairs. We have some celebrating to do."

Tess allowed herself to be pulled to her feet. She clamped down her emotions and, with Fiona's help, prepared for the feast being held in her honor. Tonight, she would smile and show her appreciation for this family that had taken her in.

Tomorrow, after she started her journey south, she knew she would have plenty of time to grieve.

Dinner at Benmore Castle was a grand affair.

The castle servants bustled about, people talked and laughed at the tables, children danced to the music and ran about after the dogs. Alexander and James were in constant conversation with the clan folk. The laird and his wife were perfect hosts. But since the start of dinner, Tess had been unmindful of everything and everyone but the handsome and exceptionally quiet young man seated beside her.

This was their last night together—the last moments. But neither of them had said much. Tess was terrified even to glance in his direction. She hadn't left, but already she was missing him. Her tears were plenty and she was holding them back only with great difficulty.

A serving man removed a platter of food that she'd left untouched before her and replaced it with an assortment of fruit.

"Not hungry tonight?" Colin asked.

Tess tried to regain her poise and find the voice to answer him, but all she was able to do was shake her head.

"Not thirsty either?" He leaned near her to check her cup. The brush of his hair against her cheek made Tess shiver. "What are you drinking, anyway?"

Tess wrapped her hand around the cup. "Water."

"Not much nourishment, considering the long days of travel ahead."

He didn't have to remind her. Her chin started trembling, and she thought her composure was about to crumble. Tess started to raise her cup to hide her sadness behind it. Colin's large hand closed over hers, his fingers holding hers captive, while his other hand filled her cup from a pitcher. "Are you cold?"

"Not cold. Sad." Heat rose into her face at the blurting out the truth of her feelings. In spite of it, Tess dared herself to look at him. His eyes were smoldering embers. "I'm leaving in the morning, and that leaves so little time to say goodbye to those I have come to care for."

"This does not have to be a final farewell." Colin reached up and casually pushed a loose strand of hair from her cheek. His fingers scorched her skin where they brushed so lightly against her face.

"I...I have little hope of ever coming back." Embarrassed at her own boldness, at sounding as if she was coaxing an invitation, Tess quickly tore her gaze from his face and stared down at weave of the cloth on the table. She loved him so much that it hurt. But her pride would not let her fall apart. She would not beg for his affection. "They say one path always leads on to other paths."

She blinked hard, forcing back the tears that were standing out in her eyes.

"Did you get a chance to meet the men your mother has send to escort you?"

She was grateful for the change in topic of conversation. "I did."

"Do you know them? Have you met them before?"

She shook her head, keeping her gaze on the table.

"Wouldn't you prefer to have someone you know accompany you?" Colin gently lifted her chin. "Someone you trust and perhaps even care for? Someone who is eager to meet your mother so he might seek her approval of him? Wouldn't you prefer someone like that to escort you to the Borders?"

Tess couldn't ignore the sudden thundering of her heart. "Are you… are you offering your services?"

He gently wiped a droplet from her cheek. "I am, if you'll have me."

She laughed through the tears. "Nothing would make me happier."

"Are you sure you don't want us to follow them?" Alexander asked. He and James and the laird stood on the battlements of the castle and watched the group of Burnett men, accompanied by Tess and Colin and only a half-dozen Macphersons, departing for the Borders. "What he's getting himself into may be far more dangerous than being washed off the deck of a ship."

"He'll be fine," the laird said, looking after the company riding down the hill from the castle.

"But you saw for yourself how surly those bloody Burnetts were last night," Alexander argued, "when they saw how Colin and Tess looked at one another."

"We know he wants to handle this on his own," James chimed in. "But he'll be outnumbered the minute they leave Macpherson land. And even if they make it to the Borders, what if Lady Evelyn doesn't fancy him coming along? The bloody witch could throw him into her dungeon or—"

"I thought you two were looking forward to being rid of him?"

"We're serious, father." Alexander cast another tense glance in the direction of the travelers.

"Very well, lads, but Colin wanted it this way. He wanted Tess's mother to see him not as a threat. He is truly hoping to gain her trust…

for the lassie's sake."

"But what if things do not go as he's planned?"

"Then we take her castle down, stone by stone."

In spite of the seriousness of the laird's tone, it was obvious that neither of the two younger men felt comfortable with the idea of waiting.

"I know what you two are thinking. You're wondering where the harm is in following along? We could be there, nearby, if Colin needs us."

Alexander and James both nodded wholeheartedly.

"But that won't be allowing him to make his own decisions. He's a man now and entitled to make his own mistakes." Alec Macpherson put a hand on each of his sons' shoulders and turned them toward the circular stair that led into the keep. "But I'd prefer that you *not* bring this up with your mother."

CHAPTER 15

The Burnett warriors were indeed a surly group, and their hostility grew less veiled the farther they traveled from Benmore Castle.

Colin couldn't care less, though, for he and Tess had chosen their own pace for most of the day, forcing the Lowlanders to slow down. But with nightfall approaching, Colin sent a couple of his own men ahead with several of the Burnetts in search of a suitable place to settle down until morning. As they waited for the scouting group to return, they continued on slowly.

Despite their apprehension over meeting with Evelyn in only a few days time, Tess and Colin had had a truly enjoyable day. He had told her much of the history of the Highlands as they had passed across the lands of the clans. She had questioned him about ways that she could bring more prosperity to people of the Lindsay clan. The conversation had turned to family. Colin had told Tess about his own immediate family.

"I am ashamed to think how little I know about my own kin," Tess said. "Lord Alec told me that my father had no siblings and that both his parents were gone before I was ever born. And I know now that my mother was from the Fleming family, of the Borders." She lowered her voice and glanced wearily at the company of Lowlanders riding at some distance ahead of them. "But as far as the family connection between the Flemings and the Burnetts, I don't remember anything of them."

Colin nodded. "My mother mentioned that there are Flemings on both sides of the Tweed, in the Lowlands and the hills of the Borders... and in England, as well. And what my father remembers of Edward Fleming, your grandfather, is that he had five daughters. Before his death, he managed to arrange profitable marriages for all of them."

"I do vaguely remember Lady Evelyn speaking of her older sisters.

There were times, I think, when she missed them badly. But I believe she also resented them for having either English husbands or husbands from the Borders." Tess shook her head sadly. Since that morning at Ravenie Castle, the lost pieces of her childhood memory kept falling into place. It was like an intricate puzzle. The more pieces she added, the clearer the solution became. "'Tis upsetting to think of my mother's prejudice against the Highlanders. I cannot believe she ever gave her new people...or her husband...a chance."

"People change." Colin pushed his horse nearer hers and affectionately took Tess's hand. "She has been living under the protection of this man, her cousin...this David Burnett...for eleven years now. He must be a good and honorable man to shoulder such a responsibility. Evelyn very well could be a different person than the one you remember. Greet with her with an open mind, Tess. Give her a chance."

Her eyes, dark and beautiful, glowed with newfound hope when she smiled at him. "All I have to say, though, is that she'd better treat you well. If she doesn't, she'll learn quickly how much *I* have changed."

Colin couldn't stop himself. He leaned over and kissed her, and the reins slipped forgotten through his fingers.

The sound of approaching horses jarred them back to reality. He drew back and looked along the ridge on which they were traveling. The group of men who'd ridden ahead were cantering back to the main party. He glanced over at Tess. A deep blush had spread over her perfect skin. Colin brought her fingers to his lips and smiled.

"We have found a place," came the shout from a Burnett warrior. Colin and Tess both turned to look at the man.

The place they had found was a deserted cottage beside a loch. A pine forest to the south of the place would provide wood for their fires and a windbreak besides. Tess would sleep in the cottage, such as it was, while everyone else could camp by the edge of the forest.

As they descended into the glade where the small cottage sat, Colin ordered his own men to join with the Burnetts in setting up a watch on two small hills overlooking the area. He hadn't expected the place to be so isolated, and the mist rising from the loch did nothing to dispel the feeling of gloom that pervaded the abandoned farm. But night was already upon them, and there wasn't any time to search out a better place.

Colin dismounted and surveyed his surroundings. As confident as he'd been before in not asking for more Macphersons to accompany them to the Borders, he was now having his doubts. In another day they'd be out of the Highlands, and Tess's account of coming face to face with her father's murderer kept echoing in his mind. It was possible that the murderer was still out there. Perhaps he had even heard that Tess was alive. He could be biding his time, waiting for the right moment to cause Tess harm. Between the Macphersons and Burnetts, there were plenty of men to defend her, but Colin didn't know much about either the courage or the fighting ability of these Lowlanders.

Some of the men had already started fires and were setting up camp by the trees. Colin helped Tess down from her horse and asked her to stay with the others as he went inside to check the cottage.

There was a door and a narrow window in the front of the place. The walls appeared solid enough. A hole in the thatched roof served to let out the smoke from an open fire pit in the center of the packed dirt floor. Colin started a fire immediately, for the cottage was damp and cold. With the exception of a pile of old straw in the corner, there was nothing else in the building.

"Are you sure you don't want to stay here with me?"

Colin turned to find Tess standing by the door. She looked bone tired, and he had a feeling her question was not intended to tease him. He sensed she was genuinely uncomfortable about this place.

"Do you feel it, too?" he asked, looking at her.

"'Tis just that...I don't know what I'm feeling," she murmured, stepping in as a loud rumble of thunder rolled in across the hills. "'Tis not as if we haven't been alone before. On the Isle of May, we managed to sleep—"

"I know. But there are too many men here who will happily carry back to your mother any story that might smack of impropriety." He looked at her and tried very hard to sound reassuring. "I'll be right outside of your door. Just call me if you need me."

She nodded with a sigh of resignation and leaned her back against the wall. He went outside and carried back a couple of blankets. She insisted on making up her own bedding, and then she refused any supper. Right after Colin kissed her goodnight, though, and turned to leave the cottage, she touched his arm. "You *will* be near."

"I'll be here just outside the threshold." He pointed, but the look of nervousness in her face was obvious. "Is there something that you are not telling me?"

She shook her head. "I'm just tired."

Colin kissed her again and went to his place outside the door.

Tess walked blindly, feeling before her as she pushed ahead. Through spider webs and mists, she moved, her fingers touching the rough stone walls and the places where something cold and wet and unidentifiable oozed down the rock. More and more, she began to find doors on every side of her. But none of them would budge, no matter how hard she pushed at them. They felt like thick slabs of wood fixed by some ogre king in a cave wall of solid rock.

The air in the corridor was growing increasingly musty and dense. Globs of wet grit dripped off the ceiling onto her hair and face. As she pushed on, a sense of panic was gradually governing her movements. Her fingers scratched at the walls. She was growing desperate for any opening, but there was nothing. Her breathing was becoming labored. The corridors seemed to be growing narrower the farther she moved in. But she couldn't stay still. She couldn't go back. The place had the feel of a grave, but there seemed to be no escape.

Blackness enveloped her, and she suddenly had no idea if she was standing or lying down. There was no up. No down. She was floating

And then Tess saw the sliver of light coming through what looked to be a wooden door straight ahead. Oriented once again, she rushed toward it, but the walls continued to close in. Stones and mud were now showering her as she ran, pelting her. She ignored the bruising of her face—the pain in her hands as she tried to push past the walls and reach the door.

And then she was before it.

The light of a brilliant sun poured through the crack in the door. Warmth emanated from the very surface of the wood. Tess saw the latch and reached for it. It, too, was warm. Lifting the latch, she began to push the door open.

Do not go inside!

The shout of warning echoed off the walls...or was it from somewhere inside her own head? It was a voice she knew. But the light seemed to be drawing her on. She was cold. She was frightened. She needed to escape this nether world, this grave. She stared at her own fingers clutching desperately to the latch.

"But I need the light...to find my way!" Her voice was small and hollow in the dark.

You can find your way without it. You can, Tess.

Her fingers dropped to her sides. She took a step back. Her gaze was drawn to the latch. It had started to glow in the darkness. She took another step backward. The door started swinging open on its own. When it was open wide, she could see the distant light shining at the end of the long tunnel. The walls beyond the door were smooth. Tess took another step back as she saw the light moving closer. Faster and faster it came, growing in intensity with each passing moment.

It was growing warmer. She was burning. The light continued to come, but she couldn't back away fast enough. Her back banged hard against a wall, and she gasped as the light transformed into a ball of fire, hurtling toward her.

Tess sat up and stared into the blanket of darkness around her. She couldn't catch her breath. Shivers racked her body, and yet she was covered in sweat.

At first, she didn't know where she was and then, as the dream receded, she remembered the cottage, the camp. Colin had promised to be right outside. She scrambled to her feet. She didn't stop to pick up her cloak. She just knew she had to get out of this place. She had to run. Tess stumbled over the blankets, but managed to right herself before she reached the door.

She slipped out into the night, but Colin was not by her door. A new wave of panic seized her, and she felt the taste of bile rising in her throat. She had to get out of this place. She had to run.

Run. The same familiar voice pounded in her head. *Run.*

She saw the gleaming waters of the loch and raced toward it. Down through the meadow she went, following a ditch and keeping her eye on the loch. As she passed a grove of trees, a pair of strong hands seized Tess from behind. She fought against him, but just as she was about to scream, she recognized the hushed whisper. Colin. She turned in his arms.

"What is it, Tess?" He touched her face, her arms. "You're shaking. What happened?"

She shook her head and a sob rose in her throat. "I couldn't find you," she whispered. "I couldn't find my way."

He wrapped an arm around her shoulder and walked her toward the loch. "I thought I heard something…or someone…by the horses. I went to look and then saw you run this way." At the stony edge of the loch, he knelt down and trailed his hand in the water.

"You are burning." He ran his wet hand over her face. Tess welcomed the bracing feel of the water, but even more so, she cherished his touch.

A crackling hiss drew their attention back toward the cottage, and they stared uncomprehendingly for a long moment. The cottage was on fire.

Colin drew his sword and pushed Tess behind him as a handful of riders broke out of the woods near the cottage and raced past the burning building. As they rode, some shot flaming arrows through the window and into the doorway, while others dropped bundles of sticks in front of the door. Soon, those too had been torched, and the building became a blazing inferno.

Those in the camp were up and running after the retreating riders, while others were rushing toward the cottage. But before they could do anything, the roof of the cottage caved in and moments later the walls began to collapse inward. Flames and sparks of yellow and gold climbed high into the night sky.

The scene before her was unreal. Tess sat in a heap on the stones at the side of the loch. How close she had come to being caught inside of the burning building, perhaps even shot by a burning arrow. She saw it in her mind…like a fireball, the arrow hurtling toward her.

Tess looked around for Colin. Two Macpherson warriors, standing with their weapons drawn, were standing near her. But Colin was up by the burning cottage, shouting orders to the Burnetts and the Macphersons. There seemed to be no sign of the outlaws. They had disappeared into the night with the same speed that they had materialized.

A few minutes later, Tess saw Colin coming across the field to her, and she pushed herself to her feet. Instead of saying anything, he simply pulled her tightly into his arms and held her for the longest time.

"That was too close. Propriety be damned, I am not letting you out of my sight until we arrive at Ninestane Castle."

"Who were they?"

"The Burnetts think they were just outlaws." He cupped her face and looked into her eyes. "But you saw what happened. I think they were after *you*, Tess."

She shivered uncontrollably.

"If you feel strong enough, I'd like to get moving now. If these bastards are watching us, which I assume they are, 'twill not take them long to realize you weren't hurt or killed in the attack. We won't be caught in such an unprotected place again."

"I am fine." She mustered all of her strength, and took another look at the dying bonfire that was once a cottage. "I have been given another chance. I don't want to waste it."

CHAPTER 16

T ired and cold from the falling rain, the travelers first saw the tower at twilight rising drearily above the brown River Tweed. Ninestane Castle, situated on a muddy pile of rock at a bend in the river, did not present a picture of hospitality in the increasing gloom, and the impression only served to heighten Tess's anxiety.

They had ridden for so long and so hard that Tess could not tell the difference between her legs and the saddle. She was soaked to the skin from the days of steady rain. She was tired and hungry. But as determined as she was to get this meeting behind her, she reined in her horse on the last hill and looked at the scenery before her. The countryside was soggy and the ground brown and slick with mud. The tower, rising above the curtain wall, was gray and forbidding.

Tess rubbed her hand across her stomach to ease the tight knot that had gripped her insides for days.

"How are you bearing up?" Colin asked, bringing his own horse to a stop beside her.

"I don't know." She couldn't tear her gaze away from the formidable structure. "I suppose I'm frightened."

"She is your mother, Tess. How could she not love you?"

She frowned, realizing there were no excitement left in her. Only apprehension.

"No battle cry has been sounded, and yet you are armed and ready," he told her with a smile. He ran a finger gently over her cheeks, brushing away the droplets of rain.

There were calls from the group that there were riders from the castle approaching. Resigned to face what lay ahead, Tess rode beside Colin and was soon greeted by a larger group of Burnetts. These people were no more cordial than the ones she had been riding beside for what felt like an eternity. With an encouraging nod from Colin, she again pushed ahead.

As they passed through a small village huddled against the curtain wall of the castle, Tess couldn't help but notice the ramshackle condition of the houses. The threadbare group of villagers they passed stood in the rain and gawked at Tess and Colin and the Macphersons, surrounded by the Burnetts as if they were a captured enemy. Tess looked into the thin, haggard faces, and she knew that she wasn't going to like this David Burnett.

So much of what she saw here reminded Tess of what she'd seen in the faces of Lindsays. There was no doubt in her mind that this same man must have been responsible for employing Flannan to manage Ravenie Castle and its holdings.

Urging her mount up the slippery mud path to the castle, Tess's distress continued to grow. Lady Evelyn had always complained of her husband and her life in the Highlands, and yet this seemed infinitely worse.

There was so much of her mother that she needed to understand.

"Please stay close to me until we at least see Lady Evelyn."

Colin obviously shared her concern. Tess nodded to him and continued up the short hill to the drawbridge spanning the pit that surrounded the castle wall.

Inside the walls of the old fortress, she peered about nervously at what looked to be dozens of armed Burnetts standing guard. Despite the rain, torches had been lit and the smoky fires filled the confines of the small courtyard. Tess suddenly felt smothered.

A set of wooden steps led from the muddy courtyard to the main entrance of the keep, and she and Colin brought their horses to a halt near it.

"I believe we have arrived." Colin said brightly, obviously trying to ease the tension. Tess didn't miss the way his sword sat loosely on his back, though, or the way the daggers at his belt and in his boot were close at hand. She knew, however, that there was not much the handful of them could do against this army of men. She placed her hands on his shoulders as he helped her down from the horse. Her feet sank up to her ankles in the mud.

Colin must have seen her first, and Tess followed the direction of his gaze. The willowy woman stood just under the overhang of the main entrance, her hands folded tightly at her waist.

A feeling of joy rushed through Tess. Eleven years of separation meant nothing, and she was once again a young child hungry for her mother's affection...and for her approval. Tess forced herself to be dignified, though, and she started toward the steps.

Despite the mantle of fur around her shoulders, Lady Evelyn was still as thin as Tess remembered her. She couldn't see her mother's eyes or the expression on her face. She had to hold a hand above her face to block the rain to continue looking up at her mother.

"Welcome, Theresa Catherine. So you have *finally* come." Something in the woman's tone made Tess pause before taking the first step. It lacked any hint of joy, and there was a waver in it that made Tess think that perhaps she was afraid. But afraid of what? Of Colin? Of Tess herself?

She stood for a moment and stared up at the woman and then glanced at Colin, who was still waiting to be recognized.

"What are you waiting for? You will come into the Hall." Without waiting for them, Evelyn turned and disappeared through the door.

Disappointment slapped Tess across the face. The happiness of a moment ago soured in her throat.

"Let's go inside." Colin murmured in her ear. Taking her by the arm, he encouraged her up the steps.

A spiral stairwell inside took them up to the Great Hall of Ninestane Castle. It was a high, wood-paneled chamber with a great fire burning in a fireplace at one end of the room. Servants moved about the smoky hall, and a half dozen armed Burnett warriors glared at the Highlander. A few feet from their mistress, a number of ladies-in-waiting watched attentively. Evelyn, however, was standing alone by the dais when Colin and Tess crossed the room.

"Jenny will take you to your bedchamber, Theresa. You can clean and change for dinner." Dismissing her with a wave of her hand, Evelyn indicated that Tess was to follow a servant who stepped forward. She turned to Colin next. "You will take your men around to the west wing to the kitchen. You all will be fed, and then you will start back to the Highlands...tonight."

Tess shook off her shock at the abrupt treatment and spoke up as brightly as she could. "Mother, 'tis wonderful to see you after so many years." She took Colin's arm and presented him. "Please allow me to present Colin Macpherson, the youngest son of Lord Alec Macpherson and Lady Fiona Drummond Stewart. He is the brave nobleman who found me on the Isle of May."

Lady Evelyn looked coolly from one to the other for a long moment.

"If you think there is a reward to be collected, Highlander," Evelyn said shortly, "you are mistaken. Sir David sent enough men to escort my daughter back. 'Twas at your own choice to travel so far—"

"M'lady, he is *not* here to collect any reward," Tess shot back. Her greatest fears had materialized. "'Twas because of this man and his family's compassion and generosity that I stand before you now. I owe him my life." She sensed Colin was about to make an objection, so she looped her hand through his arm and held it tightly. "He is not here to be paid for anything he has done. He is here because he cared enough to come and make certain I am safely settled. He is my friend, and it gave me great pleasure to know that you would have an opportunity to meet him, too."

There was an instant of silence as all color drained from her mother's face.

"You are speaking nonsense, Theresa Catherine. Befriending a Highlander!" She looked with disdain at Tess's wet and muddy attire. "Up to your room this instant. I want you out of those filthy clothes. Already you are a disappointment. I can see I shall have a lifetime of instructing ahead of me to correct all that you are lacking."

Tess stared with disbelief at the thin and rigid figure by the dais.

Colin spoke his first words since arriving in the hall. "If you will give us a moment, m'lady, perhaps we can start over. You'll be pleasantly surprised at how accomplished your daughter is...in spite of...nay, because of her time on the island."

"Accomplished in what way? In shearing sheep, mending a fishing net, being a simpleton? I read the letter you people sent me. She is obviously incapable even of exercising good judgment."

"And how capable *you* are of good judgment!" Colin fired back. "To make such a detailed assessment of your daughter with just a moment's look and a few exchanged words." He shook his head. "If your idea of accomplishment consists of insensitivity and arrogance, how fortunate Tess is that fate plucked her from your bosom at such a tender age. Aye, she was indeed blessed."

"Who are you to speak to me!" Evelyn whispered furiously.

Tears then splashed onto the woman's eyes, but she did not wipe them away. She turned from Colin and fixed her gaze on the floor at her daughter's feet. Once again attuned to her mother's ways, Tess watched Evelyn's temper turn to sorrow.

"I cannot believe I am to be treated so heartlessly. A grieving mother. My life shattered by the belief that her only child was lost...forever. The endless nights of prayer and anguish. The days of lonely reflection. The loss of hope. The despair that I should be the only one left." She turned tearful, accusing eyes on Tess. "And then the news that you were alive. And what do you do? Instead of coming directly to your own kin...

to your mother…you decide to go and hold court with strangers in the Highlands. You chose them over me. And then…then you expect me, your mother, at my age and in my condition to come and pay homage to you."

"M'lady, 'twas not like that!" Tess blurted out. "'Twas not out of disrespect that you were invited there."

"If you hear me for a moment," Colin added calmly, "you will understand that I recommended that Tess come to Benmore Castle first, in part because we did not know where you were residing at present. As your daughter says, there was no disrespect intended."

"Say what you will, I have been deeply wounded."

Tess opened her mouth to say more, but Evelyn raised a hand for silence and turned sharply to Colin.

"Sir, you have done your duty and delivered my daughter safely to me. Now, you will take your leave immediately. I have no wish to be disturbed any longer by the presence of filthy Highlanders in Ninestane Castle."

Having dismissed him, she turned back to her daughter.

"And you, Theresa Catherine, are now under my protection. You will do as I see fit. And just so that you understand the magnitude of my disappointment, my plan has been to present you at Court and negotiate a suitable marriage on your behalf. But that can only happen after you have been properly instructed in the ways of the gentility. And 'tis abundantly clear to me that Sir David and I have a great deal of work ahead of us."

"But Mother, I—"

"That is the end of this discussion. You *will* do as you are told. I will receive you in my chambers once you changed into more suitable attire. Say goodbye to your Highlander. You shall not be seeing him again."

With a withering glance at Colin, Lady Evelyn turned and glided from the hall.

Angry and frustrated, Colin ran a weary hand over his face and stared after the woman. This was not exactly how he'd imagined this meeting would go. The setback of not being able to explain everything properly had his blood boiling.

By the saints, he thought, he hadn't helped any by losing his temper with the woman, either. He was clearly the devil himself, as far as Tess's mother was concerned, and he was at a loss regarding how to remedy that now.

"That is *not* the way I imagined things would go." Tess's sad whisper drew his attention. Her face was flushed. Her beautiful eyes were brimming with tears. "Will you ever be able to forgive me for bringing you into the midst of it?"

"I wanted to come. And now, more than ever before, I am glad that I was here." He gently touched her face.

"I remember *everything* about her now, Colin," she said in a low voice. "I don't want to stay here. I want to go back to Ravenie. That is where I belong. Will you take me back to the Highlands with you?"

"I will." By the main entrance to the hall, a dozen Burnetts had taken up their positions. He remembered the army of them in the courtyard. They would have no chance of fighting their way out. "There are complications that we need to straighten out, though."

He glanced again at the door. Tess's eyes followed the direction of his look.

"You must stay here tonight with your mother. Perhaps if you were to speak to her again when things are calmer...once I've left the castle."

"And where will you be?"

The servant who was supposed to escort Tess upstairs moved nearer to them. There was no doubt in Colin's mind that everything that was said here between them would be reported to Lady Evelyn.

"I'll return to the Highlands."

Tess bit her lip, but a sob escaped nonetheless. He pulled her tightly into his arms.

His words were a rough whisper in her ear. "I shall somehow get a message to you, tomorrow or the next day at the latest. I'll not leave the Borders without you, even if I have to lay siege to this castle myself."

Tess gave a small nod, but when they pulled out of the embrace, the sadness was still there.

CHAPTER 17

Jenny, the serving woman, was small and thin and spoke scarcely two words as she led Tess up a winding stone stairwell to the bedchamber where she was to stay.

"They'll bring up yer things." The servant retreated unceremoniously toward the door.

"Will someone come after me to show me the way to Lady Evelyn's room?" Tess called after the woman.

"She'll send for ye when she wants ye," the older woman said curtly from the landing. Without another word, she disappeared down the steps.

Tess wondered if anyone would really try to stop her if she were to run down these same steps and out to the courtyard. Perhaps Colin had not yet left. Going quickly to the door, she stopped as the sound of footsteps reached her ears. A second later, two large men come around the bend of stairs. One was carrying her small trunk. The other stopped and placed the torch he was carrying in the wall sconce on the landing. He didn't move even after the first one had wordlessly dropped Tess's things in her room and walked past her at the door and down the stairs.

The guard looked at her without any feeling. She was being held prisoner.

Colin's promise of sending word—of not going back to the Highlands without her—was Tess's only source of hope as she closed the door to her small room.

The only furniture in the room was the bed, and a narrow archer's slit in the wall served for a window. The opening was covered with a piece of skin that flapped in the chill breeze. The wood floor was not even covered with rushes.

Tess had taken one step toward her trunk when she heard a bar drop in a latch on the outside of her door. She whirled and tried to pull the door open, but to no avail.

Her mother was indeed keeping her prisoner.

"Are the Highlanders gone?"

"They are, m'lady. And just as ye ordered, a company of Sir David's men are following them to make sure they're not hanging about without ye knowing."

"Very well. Now, then, I want you to take her some food." Evelyn spoke impatiently to Jenny as she sat before the large looking glass while another maidservant brushed her hair. "And see to it that she has a brazier for her bedchamber and water for washing…if she asks for it."

"She was asking to see ye," Jenny said.

"Harder. Brush harder," Evelyn ordered, ignoring the comment.

"She thinks ye'll be sending for her this night," the serving woman persisted.

"Well, she is wrong. I won't be having anything to do with her until Sir David gets back." Evelyn worriedly touched the dark circles under her eyes. There were grim lines turning down the corners of her full lips. Her jaw was taut. Her pale blue eyes seemed to have lost their luster. She looked old, and it was Theresa's fault.

"What should I be telling her?"

"That she is being punished for her heartless behavior toward me." Evelyn met the old servant's gaze in the mirror. "Tell her that all mercy lies in the hands of Sir David Burnett. Tell her that she should work on improving her manner for when she meets him."

"How about if I just tell her that yer ladyship will send for her when ye're ready?"

Evelyn turned sharply in her seat to scold the old woman, but Jenny quickly slipped from the room.

"The devil take you, too," she said harshly. "Just wait until Sir David hears about your insolence!"

The thin gray light of dawn filtered through the narrow window, and Tess drew her knees tighter to her chest. An untouched trencher of food sat on the trunk at the foot of the bed. The traveling clothes that she'd washed the mud from herself hung from a single peg on the wall. Neither the chamber pot nor the basin of water that she'd used to wash up had been removed from the room.

Last night, Tess had waited until long after all the noises of the castle had died away before giving up hope on Evelyn sending for her. And for the rest of the night, she had lay awake on the narrow bed, staring vacantly at the red glow of dying embers in the brazier and trying to make some sense out of her situation.

During her years on the Isle of May, she hadn't been able to remember her childhood. But now she had a clear recollection of how things had been. Her nurse Elsie had been the one in charge of raising Tess. Lady Evelyn's role had been to scold, to correct, to be critical of everything and everyone around her, and to list Sir Stephen's numerous flaws daily to the young Tess. Her mother had been unhappy then, and Tess guessed that not much had changed in her mother over the years.

But what were they going to do to her now? What was the reason for locking her up like this? Jenny and another servant had brought the food and water and brazier to the room last night. Neither had said a word. Jenny had refused to answer any of Tess's questions.

Her greatest worry lay with Colin. What if they had imprisoned him in the same way that they had locked her away? Even worse, what if they had hurt him?

A heavy door squeaked on old hinges somewhere down the steps. A few moments later, she heard snatches of a conversation outside her door. Quietly, Tess placed her feet on the cold wood floor and stared anxiously at the door.

After what seemed like an eternity, a bar lifted on the far side. Tess stood as the door swung open just enough for Jenny to enter. The heavy oak door banged shut behind her.

The woman was carrying a single platter that she placed next to the untouched trencher from last night. She made her way around the room, checking the chamber pot, adding a block of peat to the small brazier.

"Good morning," Tess offered, knowing that, despite her own frustration, this woman was not the cause of her troubles.

Instead of answering her, the servant cast a furtive glance at the door and made a gesture that someone might be listening there. Tess's spirit lifted as she realized that she might have an ally, after all, at Ninestane Castle. While fanning the flame in the brazier, the woman motioned to her to speak. Tess nodded her understanding.

"Look," she said loudly, "I've waited long enough. Why are they holding me like this?"

"I cannot say, mistress," the servant replied before dropping her voice to a whisper. "Yer Highlander's back. He sends word that he will be waiting for ye, tomorrow at dawn, past the village and up the river a wee bit…at the place where ye first stopped when ye saw the castle."

"But how will I get out of here?" Tess whispered back.

"Ye and I will be changing places when I bring yer food in the morning. The guard who'll be watching tonight—" She pointed at the door. "—he's fond of his ale and his sleep. And this early in the morning, no one will stop ye if ye go down the stairs, out through the kitchens and head straight for the village. Servants and workers go back and forth all the time this early in the morning."

"Bless you, Jenny." Tess clutched the old woman's hand. "Is there anything I can do for you."

"I've been paid well already by yer Highlander, mistress. Also, I have been with yer mother long enough to know ye'll be far better off far away from here." The old woman's face grew serious. "For sure, though, ye'll be wanting to be out of here before Sir David arrives. The master can be a fierce one, and I'm thinking ye'll not be liking him one bit."

"She is Theresa, I tell you. The creature *is* my daughter."

"And?" Sir David Burnett asked casually, eying Evelyn, who was pacing impatiently before him. The Lowlander had arrived at sunset—a day earlier than expected—but before he could settle down for his supper, he was told that Lady Evelyn needed to have a private audience with him immediately.

"Do as you have to do to her," she ordered sharply, turning to him. "She is like her filthy father—in looks, in manners, in her arrogance. Send her to hell, for all I care!"

"Things are no longer so simple," he said thoughtfully, scratching his beard.

"Then *make* it simple," she replied haughtily. "And do it now, as I don't want to hear from her, see her, or have anything to do with her. I couldn't sleep last night. And all day I have been having visions of that brute Stephen, appearing from nowhere before me. Bury her alive. Drown her if you wish, but—"

David's grip was bruising when it clamped around Evelyn's wrist. With a single movement, he yanked her against him.

"Watch your tongue," he growled into her face. "You are behaving like a madwoman. I'll have no talk of dead men appearing. And I tell you, after your reception of the Macpherson lad yesterday, you could find my head on a spiked pole with that kind of talk."

"That filthy Highlander deserved to be..."

"That filthy Highlander happens to be a cousin of the queen herself. That filthy Highlander is a scion of the most influential clans in Scotland."

"How dare you treat me like this!" she hissed, pulling away from him. "But it doesn't make one bit of difference, does it? She was better off on that island. But now that she is here, she must *never* leave. And we both know why."

David looked closely into her face. "Nothing can happen to her while she is under my protection."

"What do you mean?" Evelyn seethed through clenched teeth. "Would you like me to send for her now? Do you have any doubt that she will recognize the face of her father's murderer?"

Tess ceased her pacing when she heard the footsteps coming up the stairwell. A moment later the latch lifted.

Jenny slipped inside, carrying a clean chamber pot. Immediately, Tess knew that something was wrong when the old woman motioned for them to get away from the door.

"He's here, mistress. He and his men returned an hour ago."

"Sir David?" Tess asked, and the servant nodded nervously. She had so many questions, but she knew this was not the time to ask them. Things like, how could possibly Sir David's treatment of her be any worse than her mother's?

"Ye had better leave tonight. There's no telling where he'll move ye from here or who he'll put to keep watch." Her voice hushed even more, and the old woman's eyes showed her genuine fear. "He is a devil in ways ye don't know, mistress. Tomorrow could be too late."

"You said Colin will meet me at dawn. Can I leave the castle, get through the gates tonight?"

"Aye…if ye hurry. I don't know if yer man'll be there now or meet ye there in the morn, but spending a night in the woods would be far safer than waiting here."

Jenny's nervousness was rubbing off on Tess. While the servant rattled off the layout of the castle, the two of them hurriedly exchanged their clothes.

"Are you sure they won't do anything to you?" Tess asked as Jenny pushed the full chamber pot into her arms and pulled the kerchief lower on Tess's forehead.

"Nay, miss." She picked up the wash basin. "By the time they come in, I'll have a fine welt where ye dinged me with this. 'Twas all yer doing."

Jenny tapped on the door and pulled quickly back. Tess's heart was lodged in her throat when the door opened a crack and a tall warrior peered down at her. She held the chamber pot up and looked back at Jenny as the man let her through.

She didn't even pause to take a breath on the landing. Peering through the darkness past the single torch on the wall, she brushed past the guard and moved silently down the narrow set of stairs. A few steps down, she heard voices at the bottom of stairs and nearly tripped, but she caught the pot at the last minute and continued on.

Reaching an arched doorway at the bottom, she saw a door that she remembered Jenny said led outside. As she was ready to run for it, though, she leaped back, flattening herself against the wall when a portly servant walked in, carrying a tray heaped with food.

"About bloody time ye showed up!" the man complained loudly. "Ye take up this food with the others. Now ye give that to me and take this. And look sharp, hussy."

Two other servants walked in carrying wine and more food, and there was a jam in the narrow landing. A moment later, though, Tess found the tray in her hands.

"Hurry now. He doesn't like waiting."

A feeling of dread washed through her, settling like ice in her middle. The servant carrying the pitcher of wine walked before her. The other pushed her from behind with the tray she was carrying.

At that moment, Tess knew exactly how it felt to walk to the gallows.

CHAPTER 18

"Nothing can happen to her while she is under my protection," David repeated, his tone conveying the danger of his position. "The Macphersons would bring the very legions of hell to my gate. They'd accuse me of murder…and succeed in holding me responsible. We'll not take that chance."

"This is the fault of that foul Highlander. We could have claimed that she never arrived here, if it weren't for him." Evelyn glared accusingly at him. "Your men should have done away with her when they were on the road."

"They *tried*, but the accursed lass escaped the burning cottage."

They stopped speaking at the sound of a knock.

"Yer supper, Sir David," one of the servants called, pushing the door open.

Evelyn glided across the room to the window. It was already dark outside. She shivered as a cool breeze wafted in and chilled her. They had to get rid of Theresa. They had to find a way and do it soon.

It was bad enough receiving the letter that Theresa was alive. Coming face to face with her daughter last night, though, had completely unnerved her. She felt her world crumbling around her once more. Aye, it was all happening again. Eighteen years ago she had loved David Burnett, but no one had listened to her begging and crying that he was the only man that she could love. That he was the only man that she could spend the rest of her life with. It didn't matter to her that he had no wealth. He was a warrior and would earn his place in the world. Even her own sisters had sided with their father and betrayed her.

So Evelyn had gone to the Highlands bitter and resolute on the course her life would take. If she had been forced to live a life of misery, then by God there would be no peace around her. She would never be happy, and she would make certain no one around her would be happy, either.

But the misery she inflicted had not been enough. As Stephen spent more and more time in the service of his king, she started meeting secretly again with David. He still loved her. He hadn't forgotten her. He hadn't taken a wife. It was then that they had planned their scheme.

Eleven years ago, she had considered Theresa *her* child. The six-year-old was impressionable enough, and Evelyn knew she could mold the girl into anything she wished. If all had gone as they'd planned, she would have taken the child back with her to the Borders. But that had been the only portion of their scheme that had failed.

And David was certain that the child had seen his face.

Assuming that the girl was dead for all these years had been a great relief. But last night, Evelyn's world had fallen to pieces around her as she stared into the accusing eyes of her husband.

Theresa Catherine was *his* daughter. In looks and in spirit, the dead had been raised.

A tray hit the floor with a loud clatter, and Evelyn turned sharply to see the spilled food a step away from the table where David had seated himself for his supper. The clumsy servant, her head bowed over her task, was hurriedly cleaning up the mess. Another servant cursed quietly and continually at the woman and ordered the other two maids to run to the kitchens for more food.

Evelyn's gaze fixed on the servant. A lock of dark hair had escaped the kerchief. She glimpsed the fair face, the full lips, the flitting glance at David's missing fingers as he rested his hand on the edge of the table. Evelyn took a step toward the girl, but she paused as David slowly rose from his chair. His look told her that he had guessed at her identity, as well.

"I told the cook to send Jenny," the other servant continued to complain under her breath as she crouched by the girl, helping with the tray. "Don't know what he's thinking, sending new help with the master's meal. Hurry, ye fumbling puss! Out quick...and take this mess with ye."

Evelyn frowned at the two women, scrambling on their knees by the table. Theresa was wearing Jenny's dress. The old fool had taken her up to her bedchamber. She had taken her meals into her. And now she had helped the girl escape in her clothes. So even her own servants were betraying her. Evelyn felt her temper rise, and she took another step

145

toward them. Well, it would take only a moment to put a quick end to this treachery. As she opened her mouth to speak, David raised his hand and Evelyn's gaze shifted to his face. With the slightest shake of his head, he signaled for her to wait.

Theresa lifted the tray unsteadily and scurried toward the door.

"Let her go," David said quietly. "That is exactly where I want her... running after her Highlander with witnesses who will swear she stole away of her own accord. Outside of this castle, she is no longer under my protection...and then our problems are solved."

With her heart drumming in her ears, Tess raced down the steps.

He was coming after her. Him. Her father's killer. Her mother's protector. Now everything made sense. They would kill her for sure now, for she had seen it all.

But had they recognized her?

At the bottom of the stairs, she looked in confusion at the tray in her hands. She couldn't run through the yard with this. But she couldn't risk though going to the kitchens, either.

"I'll take that from ye, mistress." The woman's hushed voice behind her made Tess jump. She hadn't even realized that the other woman had followed her down the steps. "Ye run for the gate now, before they figure something's amiss."

Tess gaped at her for a moment, stunned by the servant's words. They were all against Evelyn. They all knew her for what she was. She let go of the tray when the other woman took it.

"Pull the kerchief down over yer eyes. Walk quick, and don't answer any of them curs at the gate. When ye get clear of the drawbridge, follow the road to the village, but turn right at the split in the road. From there, ye can cut over to the woods before you reach the first cottage. That'll take ye to the riverbank." The woman darted a look up the stairwell. "Run, now. I hear someone coming."

"Thank you." Tess whispered raggedly and pushed through the door the woman pointed to.

The sky was dark and heavy, but there was no rain. Tess's feet sank into the mud outside the door, but she didn't care. Only a handful of men were visible in the courtyard, and Tess was relieved to see a small group of workers crossing the yard toward the gate. She hurried to them and fell in a couple of steps behind the group. She had to stifle the urge to run. She kept her head down, but felt as if everyone in the world knew who she was.

The past twenty-four hours had given Tess a chance to come to terms with her mother's hatred. She had not caused Lady Evelyn's feelings toward her, but she was not willing to live with them, either. The last few moments, though, had revealed the horrible truth, and another powerful need had surfaced within her. Revenge. She would avenge her father's murder. But to do that, Tess first had to get away.

There were lewd calls from some of the soldiers keeping watch as Tess passed through the gate. She did as the servant told her, though, and followed the rest of the people out. Once outside the castle's curtain wall, Tess slowed down a little, giving the others an opportunity to move ahead of her.

She found the split in the road and a few moments later was moving silently across the fields toward the woods beyond. Once she'd stepped into the trees, though, the darkness became an ominous presence. Every tree and shrub threatened her. The sounds of night intimidated her.

But nothing of what lay ahead compared to the murderous monster behind her.

As she followed a path through the woods, Tess tried to gauge the direction of the river. Once she found that, she would simply follow it to the point where she was to meet Colin at dawn.

A twig cracked behind her. She turned around, but there was no one. Tess stepped out of the path and waited a moment. Nothing appeared, but prickles of vulnerability raced up and down her back. She was totally unfamiliar with her surroundings. She had no defense against anything...or anyone...that might be lying in wait in the darkness ahead.

Feeling around at her feet, she found a stick, straightened up, and started along the path again. It was all she could do to fight down her panic.

A few moments later, the sound of the river reached her ears. She stopped. Looking around her, though, she could not decide where the sound was coming from. But Tess knew that no matter how bad her confusion was, she still had to choose. It wouldn't be long before Sir David and her mother sent for her. They quite possibly had done so already and found Jenny in her place.

The sound of heavy footfalls came from behind her on the path. Someone was in the woods. Tess listened, unable to move from the spot. There were more footsteps. The sound of men whispering quietly. They were so near. The Burnetts were after her.

Before she could move, though, a thought pushed forward in her brain. Why would Sir David's men need to be quiet? Why not light torches? Send armies of people in search of her?

It could be Colin and his men. They could be hiding in these same woods. With a sense of relief that almost took her breath away, she opened her mouth to call to them…and then stopped.

Whoever it was, they were getting closer, and Tess felt the hairs on her neck stand up. Acting on instinct, she took off again through the woods, away from the sounds. Bramble bushes caught at her clothes and young saplings slapped at her face, but she didn't look back. Frantic, she charged on through the dark glade.

Tess no longer had any idea where she was or what direction she was going. Confusion surrounded her as she tore through the forest. The pulsing of her heart in her ears blocked out all noise, and it was not long before her energy started slipping away. Sobs of desperation rose into her throat, choking her. And yet, on she ran.

She didn't even see the man who stepped from behind the tree until she ran into him. His bruising fingers clamped on her arms, and Tess could feel the missing fingers on his right hand. She tried to scream, but fear and shock clawed at her throat.

"And finally we meet." He spoke quietly, without feeling. "And I am very grateful to you for making our little business so simple for me to finish this time."

Tess stared up into his dark eyes and realized she was no longer thinking of her own end. Her fear dissipated into the darkness like a puff of smoke. Instead, she found that she was filled with anger at the injustice that would never be righted.

"Why?" she said coolly. "Why did you have to kill my father? She could have walked away from the marriage. Why such cold-blooded murder?"

"He who lives by the sword, dies by the sword," Burnett answered bluntly. "The sword was Stephen's way. He was brave enough, and he was too proud to accept his wife leaving him. It would have been a blemish on his name."

"So you took his life."

"He took Evelyn against her wishes. And I took her back. It was the way he lived. It was what he knew."

"You stabbed him in the back."

Burnett looked away into the darkness. "Think me evil if you will, but there was no difference between Stephen and me. We lived our lives by the sword."

"That's a lie."

"He killed in the name of the king. I killed in the name of justice."

"And you call *this* justice?" Tess tried to shrug off his touch, but his fingers only tightened more painfully on her arms. "Chasing me through the woods. Will you stab me in the back, too, and call it justice?"

A hard smile broke on his face. "Others will see it that way after they hear that I have hung the outlaws who I will say attacked and killed young Macpherson and his men...and Evelyn's only child. There are many in Ninestane Castle who will honestly swear that a foolish lass ran off to meet with her Highland lover."

"Colin," she gasped. The taste of bile rose into her mouth.

"As we speak, my men are putting your dear Highlanders to the sword. You will be relieved to know, though, that they will die peacefully while they sleep."

Tess went wild in his arms, kicking and punching with the fury of a tiger. "I'll kill you with my bare hands if you go close to him. By St. Adrian's blood, I'll cut you into pieces and use you for fish bait if you so much as touch him."

He tried to hold her with his mutilated hand while reaching for his dagger with the other. Tess bit hard on his thumb, and he roared in pain. Angry, he slapped her hard across the face, knocking her backward. Stunned by the force of the blow, Tess fell against a tree, striking her head hard on the knobby trunk.

A million lights exploded in her head, nearly blinding her momentarily, and she felt herself sinking to the ground. The woods whirled crazily. Tess watched helplessly through the haze as the murderer pulled the dagger out of its sheath and took a step toward her.

And suddenly, there were torches coming through the trees.

"They were not there, m'lord!"

"Empty rolls of straw and blanket!"

"Not one filthy Highlander anywhere."

The urgent shouts of his men running into sight pulled Burnett's attention away.

"What do you mean, no one there?"

"Their horses were still tethered to the trees," the first one answered.

"Don't make a sound." The whisper was so low that Tess thought she had imagined it. As Burnett started shouting orders to his men, she felt strong arms wrap around her waist and drag her slowly backward. She looked over her shoulder and felt her heart soar when she realized it was Colin.

Burnett turned at that instant, and his angry roar echoed through the woods. "Stop him! Kill him!"

The Lowlanders raced toward them with their swords raised.

Tess watched in amazement as Colin's men came out of the shadows of the trees like men possessed. The first volley of arrows cut down the first line of Lowlanders, and the rest soon felt the cutting edge of Macpherson steel.

Colin, with a quick glance at Tess, turned murderous eyes on the large man who was moving toward them.

"He is the one," she managed to whisper, pushing herself upright. "He...killed my father." She fought the fog blurring her vision and tried to focus on Colin as his sword clashed with the murderer's. Sparks flew into the night as the two men fought ferociously.

Leaning her weight on the tree, Tess forced herself to her feet. *Don't let him get hurt. Please, God. Don't let any harm come to him.*

Blow after blow, the ringing sound of steel filled the glade, but then in horror she saw Colin trip. With his sword flashing upward in the torchlight, the Lowlander stepped forward to deliver the final blow. With all her strength, Tess pushed away from the tree and threw her weight against Burnett's side. He stumbled forward and fell across Colin.

Tess watched the Lowlander's body twist sharply when he hit the ground, and then lay still.

She blinked and looked over at Colin, who was on one knee and covered with blood.

And then the world went black.

CHAPTER 19

F rom the magnificent view out the high window, Tess admired the lush and fertile farm lands, the broad expanses of forest, the rocky upland moors surrounding the Border stronghold. She was in Roxburgh Castle, scarcely a two hour ride from Ninestane and a place where Colin knew she would be safe. Roxburgh belonged to Ambrose Macpherson, his uncle, Colin told her. She looked up at the clear blue sky and breathed in the fresh spring air.

"Are ye ready to take yer meal now?"

Tess turned and smiled at the housekeeper who was ushering a servant with a tray of food into the room.

"Ina, you don't need to be serving me like this. I am well enough to come and take my meals with everyone else in the Great Hall."

"Well, Master Colin's orders were for ye to follow the abbot's advice and stay in bed this week." The housekeeper started arranging the food on a table near the window. "I let ye out of bed, but ye are weak and need to get yer strength back before he returns."

Before he returns.

She loved the sound of those words. In her mind she saw him, returning from Stichel where he'd taken Lady Evelyn.

Tess stared at the distant hill. David Burnett was dead. He had died when he'd fallen on Colin's dagger. The same night, Ninestane Castle had come under siege by Colin and the company of Macphersons that he'd gathered from Roxburgh Castle. With their leader dead, there had been little resistance. But dealing with Evelyn had been more difficult. Tess's mother had become wild upon hearing the news. Crazed with grief, she would have jumped from the tower to her death if Colin hadn't physically restrained her.

Scotland's Council of Regents, in Berwick for a meeting with English officials, had decided Evelyn's fate that same week. She was to be sent away where she could bring no harm to anyone and live out the rest of her life in solitude. Evelyn herself had chosen the convent at Stichel.

Tess had been recovering at Roxburgh through all of this, and her mother refused to see her or talk to her. A stranger seemed to have inhabited Evelyn's body since Burnett's murder. She was a madwoman who claimed she'd never had either husband or daughter. But she was at peace with the sentence she'd been given. She planned to grieve her dead lover for the rest of her life.

"Now, ye don't want to get me in trouble with that handsome lad now by falling ill again, do ye?"

Tess turned away from the window and smiled at the housekeeper. "He is coming back today, isn't he?"

"That is what I hear." Ina started serving the food.

"She is not giving you any trouble, is she?"

Colin's voice made Tess cry out in joy. "You are back!"

He opened his arms, and they met in the middle of the room. He whirled her about and kissed her before she had a chance to say another word. They had only seen each other in fleeting moments this past week. And she couldn't believe how much she had missed him.

It was a long time before Tess pulled out of his embrace. She looked around the room and found Ina had already slipped out.

"Thank you...for everything." She hugged him again fiercely.

"Your mother seems comfortably settled in the convent."

"Thank you," Tess whispered sadly. "This is one part of my life that I would like to forget. I don't want to think back about my mother's deceit...about her hatefulness. I don't think I ever want to come back to the Borders again."

"I know this might surprise you, considering I am a Highlander, but there is nothing wrong with the Borders." His hand caressed her face, and his blue eyes sparkled with that roguish glint that made her heart sing. "What you need is to replace the bad memories with good ones while you are still here."

She smiled remembering their visit to Ravenie Castle and how he had enticed her through it. "Well, I already know you are an expert at that. I don't think I shall ever walk through the gates at Ravenie and not remember...you." She blushed at the thought of the way he had kissed her there. He had been so patient and supportive throughout that day.

"Perhaps we need to make a pact about this. Whenever one of us is troubled, it shall be the other's duty to bring a smile back. Whenever one is ailing, it shall be the other's responsibility to nurture them back to health. We'll make it our calling in life to create those good memories and keep them alive for each other."

Tess's heart began to beat so hard that she thought her chest would burst. "I would like that."

"Perhaps this pact should continue...indefinitely?"

She nodded once, twice, and then smiled up at him. A tear escaped, and then another. Suddenly, Tess was overwhelmed by the emotions surging within her. She quickly dashed away the tears on her face. "I love you, Colin. There is nothing that would make me happier than making this pact with you."

The Highlander lifted Tess in his arms and spun her around. "And I love you, my own. Say that you'll marry me."

"Aye, Colin. I will marry you," she whispered as he finally came to a stop. The laughter in her eyes, though, was replaced with sharp awareness as their gazes locked. "But tell me that I am not just dreaming this."

"You are not dreaming." Colin brushed his lips against hers. "You and I. Together for life. For ever and a day."

Tess wrapped her arms around his neck and returned his kisses. The happiness coursing through her was beyond anything she could have imagined. A thought struck her and she drew back a little.

"But what about your parents? Would they mind having their youngest son—"

"They already know. I was ready to pour my heart into your hands before we ever left the Highlands. But quite wisely, they suggested I should wait until your mind was settled about your mother."

She couldn't hold back her laugh. "So does this mean now that I get to meet the rest of the Clan Macpherson? I have been hearing from Ina all about your aunts and uncles and cousins—"

Colin's arms remained wrapped around her. "And friends and cousins of friends. And before our wedding, you shall certainly be obliged to meet our neighbors and the neighbors' cousins and friends of the neighbors' cousins..."

"'Tis wonderful to have so many people who love and care for you so much that they actually want to meet me."

"To be honest, they'll all be coming to warn you about the scoundrel that you are marrying."

Tess placed a kiss on his chin. "I'm sure your brothers will have more to say on that topic."

"I have an idea."

"What is it?" Tess asked.

"Before any of them arrive," Colin said, scooping her off the floor with a devilish smile. "Let's elope."

AUTHOR'S NOTE

We hope you enjoyed Tess and Colin's story. As always, we have tried to depict a place and a time in a way that mingles the real and the imagined in an entertaining way. And Scotland is such a special place. Roxburgh Castle and the Isle of May and the ruins of St. Adrian Chapel are very real places. In fact, while researching this novel, we found that St. Adrian's Chapel was recently discovered actually to be the chapel of an earlier Christian evangelist named St. Ethernan, who died in AD 669 while working among the Picts, an ancient people of Scotland who disappeared in the Middle Ages. His chapel, though, was a favorite shrine for pilgrims, visited by peasants and kings alike who traveled there hoping to be cured of all types of ailments. Today, the Isle of May is a favorite spot for day-tripping birdwatchers.

Several members of the Macpherson clan that you met in this story were initially introduced in some of our earlier adult historical romance novels. For those who are interested in seeing a family tree (of sorts), we have outlined the connections here.

We love to hear from our readers. You can contact us at:

May McGoldrick

e-mail: mcgoldmay@aol.com

The 'May McGoldrick Family Tree' Book Information

Our 16th Century books...

In *The Thistle and the Rose*, Colin Campbell and Celia Muir are introduced...

And we also introduce Alec Macpherson, who is the hero of our second book, *Angel of Skye*...

Alec has two brothers, Ambrose and John, who are the heroes of *Heart of Gold* and *The Beauty of the Mist*, respectively...

In *Angel of Skye*, we also introduce a little boy, Malcolm MacLeod, and in *Heart of Gold* we introduce a little girl, Jaime...

When Malcolm MacLeod and Jaime grow up, they are the hero and heroine of *The Intended*...

In *Heart of Gold*, we also introduce Gavin Kerr, who becomes the hero of *Flame*...

In *Flame*, we introduce a number of characters who show up in *The Dreamer*, *The Enchantress*, and *The Firebrand* (the Highland Treasure Trilogy), including John Stewart, the earl of Athol and a number of villains...

The Highland Treasure Trilogy is the story of three sisters...Catherine Percy of *The Dreamer*, Laura Percy of *The Enchantress*, and Adrianne Percy of *The Firebrand*...

In *The Enchantress*, we introduce Sir Wyntoun MacLean, who also appears in *The Firebrand*...

In *The Firebrand*, we also introduce Gillie the Fairie-Borne, who may just have a story of his own one day...

Colin Campbell and Celia (from *The Thistle and the Rose*) also make a 'cameo' appearance in *The Firebrand*...

Alec Macpherson and Fiona (from *Angel of Skye*) have three sons. The youngest, Colin Macpherson, is the hero of *Tess and the Highlander* (a young adult novel published by HarperCollins in November 2002)...

Our 18th Century Books

In *The Promise,* Samuel Wakefield, the earl of Stanmore, and Rebecca Neville/Ford are the hero and heroine...

In that book we also introduce Stanmore's friend, Sir Nicholas Spencer, who becomes the hero of *The Rebel,* which is set in Ireland...

Stanmore and Rebecca also appear in *The Rebel*...

In *The Promise,* we also introduce Rebecca's friend, Millicent Wentworth, who becomes the heroine of *Borrowed Dreams*...

Borrowed Dreams is the start of a new trilogy about three Scottish brothers, starting with Lyon Pennington, earl of Aytoun. We also meet a new cast of characters who show up in the trilogy. Violet, from *The Promise,* plays a big role in this book, too. She will show up again in the third book in the trilogy, *Dreams of Destiny.*

In *Captured Dreams,* we see Lyon and Millicent and the entire household of Baronsford in Scotland, along with wonderful heroes and villains that David Pennington meets in colonial Boston.

In *Dreams of Destiny,* the mystery of Emma's death is solved...

Visit us at www.JanCoffey.com

About the Author

NIKOO and JIM McGOLDRICK have spent their lives gathering material for their novels. Nikoo, a mechanical engineer, and Jim, who has a Ph.D. in sixteenth-century British literature, wrote their first May McGoldrick novel in 1994. Since then, they have taken their readers from the Highlands of Scotland to the mountains of Kurdistan in bestselling, award-winning historical romance and contemporary suspense novels under the names May McGoldrick, Nicole Cody, and Jan Coffey.